Asiago and the Accomplice

Judy Volhart

Published by Open Books

Copyright © 2016 by Judy Volhart

ISBN-10: 0692665803 /

ISBN-13: 978-0692665800

CHAPTER ONE

*I*n the game of life, timing is everything. Hard work too, of course, however there is so much that is out of our control. This was the turning point in my life, as I explored a new fork in my road, and I was seriously starting to doubt my decision and was feeling like I was depending entirely on fate for the next chapter of my life. I hated that weak and helpless feeling.

In contrast to the picturesque and gently falling snow, I suddenly landed hard and gracelessly on the walkway, having slipped on a patch of ice. Lying on my rump on the pathway to my new home and future bistro, I fought back the overwhelming urge to flail my limbs and wail. I gave in only briefly, jiggling one winter-boot clad foot for a few seconds.

Talking myself out of having a tantrum, I took a deep, calming breath, snorting up some big fluffy snowflakes in the process. After a brief coughing fit, I sat up to assess the damage.

Sore butt? Check.

Wheezing lungs? Check.

Sore wrist? Check. But only one. I would likely live.

Groceries? Oh yeah, all over the place.

Eggs? But of course... I'll have mine scrambled, please.

Sighing, I stood and started to repack the food into the bag. Okay, I must confess; bags which I, of course, had to attempt to carry all seven at once.

The eggs, while mostly cracked, would still make a nice meal once I salvaged what I could. See, I told myself, it's all in how you look at things, right? Broken eggs? No problem—I wanted an omelet anyway. My fall merely sped up the omelet process without having to individually crack those pesky shells. I smirked to myself, amused by my own useless pep talk.

My name is Amalia Kis. I'm five feet, nine inches tall, with brown eyes and long golden- brown hair that I like to describe as caramel-colored in an attempt to make myself sound more interesting. I'm pretty normal looking and not unusual in any way, unless you count my quirky sense of humor and complete lack of co-ordination.

I woke up one day and realized that if I was ever going to pursue my dream, no better opportunity would ever present itself, and I would surely regret it if I didn't just go for it. There was nothing to hold me back except my own fear.

About two years ago, I had finally succeeded in breaking up with my boyfriend of six years. The love had disappeared years earlier, and although I couldn't ever prove it, I was pretty sure he had cheated on me. The closest I ever came to concrete proof was finding a condom in his wallet. Since I was on birth control, and we were apparently exclusive, we never used condoms, so their mere existence in our home was as good as a guilty plea in my eyes. His excuse was classic: "Uh, I don't how it got there. It's not mine." The best part was the look he gave me, the "how can you accuse me of such a thing; I am wounded" look. Surely I should believe that it had just miraculously appeared through no intervention or will on his part.

We had owned a condo in downtown Ottawa together, as well as a car and two cats. He had a considerable amount in RRSP's (in the US, I believe this is similar to what you call a 401K) while I did not, as every extra penny I had I put into our home. I gave, he took. I cooked, he ate. I cleaned, he made a mess. I bought things for the condo, he bought things for himself.

Naturally, he never supported my dreams of opening a bistro, saying it was too risky. "It's a new concept...what if it bombs? And really, with your *condition,* you think you'd have the energy for it?" he'd asked disdainfully. I resented it immensely and yes, hated him instantly. It wasn't like I was dying or contagious, but obviously I had become inferior in his eyes. The look he gave me said it all.

After years of trying to break up, taking him back and putting my dreams on hold, I finally put my foot down after the condom discovery and the crack about my condition and stuck to it. I was twenty-eight at the time.

We had not owned the condo for long at that point, only a couple of years, so we had not paid much towards the mortgage. He declared that he wanted half its worth. I declared that I then wanted half of his RRSP's. My lawyer declared that the house was worth less than the mortgage still owing, but he was generous and rounded it up to zero. Half of zero was still zero, and my ex was welcome to it. However, half of his RRSP's would net me at least ten thousand dollars!

Needless to say, my self- centered ex quickly agreed that I could keep the condo and he would keep the car, his RRSP's and one cat. Adios. I wish I could say that I never saw him again after that, however, it took him a good eight months to clear out most of his belongings, and even then he left things behind.

To say that I struggled to pay the mortgage each month is an understatement. Although I had a good job as a manager at an insurance company and earned a good salary, downtown Ottawa was not cheap. I was determined to make it on my own however, and would never admit defeat. After all, although I am a stubborn Hungarian, my name is derived from the Germanic word "amal", which means "work". But more importantly, if my parents even sensed a hint of my struggles, they would no doubt pressure me to move back to Montreal to be closer to them. That thought alone made me shudder!

So I did what I had to do. I worked hard each day, earned a few good raises, took in a roommate and had a very minimal social life. And by minimal, I mean none. For two years. There simply wasn't any extra money to socialize.

Four months ago, the company that I worked for made a surprising announcement: lay-offs would be necessary before the end of the year. Being a manager and knowing every aspect of how my department functioned, I was sure that my job was safe.

But to everyone's shock, I volunteered. I knew that this was that opportune moment, that intervention of fate that I needed. I was given a six month severance package with full pay and benefits. At the same time, the real estate market was doing very well. I put the condo up for sale and made a bit of a profit. Leaving the rest of Hans' belongings in the dumpster on moving day was a delicious bonus.

And that leads me to the walkway on which I was still standing, looking sadly at my crushed eggs and fighting off a panic attack. Here I was. My new home. An older house, just past the edge of a busy, populated city, and at the beginning of a much smaller, cozy town. Both towns were part of the City of Ottawa, however here in the town of Robin, I was definitely in the country. Hence, my dollars went much farther.

For a very good price, I was able to purchase a home that had previously housed a struggling restaurant on the main floor and living quarters upstairs. I had big plans and a lot of work to do, and if those plans didn't take off within the next couple of months, I'd have very little money left and my severance pay would be ending. Both my home and new business were at stake, not to mention my pride.

With that reminder, I straightened my shoulders and walked around to the rear of the building to the back entrance that led to the bistro office and the kitchen. I would store most of the food down here and test out all the appliances to be sure everything was in order for opening night. I didn't want any last minute surprises. I wasn't exactly a perfectionist, but I did like to plan ahead and be prepared for any possible glitches.

I was within a few feet of the entrance when I noticed that the door's window had been smashed in. So much for wanting no surprises. Damn! Not even moved in yet and already problems. Although the house had been vacant for a while, it was still upsetting to see that it had been vandalized. My mood further soured to find that the doorknob was also broken. Okay, think positive, I told myself. My hands were full anyway, so now I wouldn't have to fumble with the lock.

I pushed the door open with my good wrist. As my eyes slowly adjusted to the change in lighting, I froze, and for the second time in only minutes, my bags crashed to the floor as I screamed and bolted back outside. I peed a little.

My mind raced, trying to assimilate what I had seen. I actually wasn't quite sure. In fact, I was probably being jittery for no reason. I peered back inside cautiously in an effort to make my eyes adjust from the bright snow outside to the darkness within.

The office space was empty except for a few boxes of what appeared to be junk, a shelving unit, my grocery bags and coat hooks bolted to the wall by the door. What looked like a giant coat was hanging from the hooks. This was what had startled me.

Satisfied that I was over-reacting and laughing

sheepishly to myself, I took a tentative step back inside, but as I drew closer I was puzzled to find that the coat was wrapped around a mop. A mop that had boots? This wasn't making any sense. What kind of joke was this? I thought for sure that my brother had arrived a day early to help me and was playing a prank. I inched closer and then recoiled in horror.

It was not a mop. It was a person with stringy grey hair. Or was it?

I bolted back outside. Peered in again. Stood motionless, waiting for something to happen. The coat, too, remained motionless. I inched closer and gently prodded it with a mittened finger. "Hello?" Nothing. Poke. Louder. "Hello?" I have no explanation as to why I spoke to it. I think I was still thinking this was a prank of some sort.

Realization and common sense clicked in at the same time. I lurched back outside while fumbling with my cell phone, dropping it in the snow. After a few tries, my hands stopped shaking long enough to dial 911. Whatever it was, it was out of my realm of expertise, but I knew damn well it wasn't a mop.

8 EGG & CHEESE QUICHE OR OMELETS
(OR 12 IF YOURS DIDN'T FALL ON THE GROUND)

1 readymade pie crust in its pan (for Quiche)
Eggs (minimum of 6)
veggies of your choice: I use 1/2 an onion, 1/2 of
each red & green pepper, handful of mushrooms,
handful of spinach, sometimes a few pieces of broccoli
and one small carrot chopped up real tiny
1 cup cheese of your choice (cheddar works well)
1/3 cup milk
Cooked bacon or any other type of already cooked
meat (sausage is good, or steak)

Use a good size skillet that will fit everything and is preferably oven-safe too. Cook all the veggies lightly in a bit of whatever oil you have. Once almost done cooking, add your chopped meat of choice to warm through.

Meanwhile, mix up your eggs with about 1/3 cup milk. Add a bit of salt and pepper (note, I also always add a bit of garlic powder (not salted) and dried dill weed to everything). Add any other herb that you like, fresh or dried.

Pour eggs over veg & meat mixture and stir quickly just to set the eggs a bit. Quickly stir in cheese of your choice, mix again quickly, then pour whole thing over your pie crust. If you're making just an omelet, see below.

Bake in over at 350 degrees Celsius until egg is set- about 30 to 45 minutes.

For a gluten-free version or if you're just making an omelet, don't use the pie crust, just put mixture into a greased round casserole dish or round baking tin (or use your oven-safe skillet).

CHAPTER TWO

The police and ambulance arrived at the same time, screeching onto the scene with lights flashing and sirens wailing, and welcoming me loudly to the town of Robin. While waiting, I had returned to my car, an old Mazda Protègé I'd gotten from my parents after the break-up, and had the creaky old heater blasting lukewarm puffs of air amidst mechanical groans of protest. I was chilled to the bone, both from the weather and the gruesome discovery.

The police jotted down the meager information I could offer. I could only confirm that I had last seen the house about a month earlier when I was allowed access to take measurements and that I was just moving a few boxes in today. I didn't know anyone in the area yet, had no enemies of which I was aware, nor did I recognize the coat.

"Ma'am, did you touch anything?"

I tried to remember. "The doorknob, but it was actually already broken, and the window was busted, too. I don't think I touched anything else, and I had on mittens. Maybe the door itself, but I didn't get more than a few feet inside the house," I said.

The cop scowled and scratched on his pad of paper. "Were you in contact with anyone outside?"

"No, I had just arrived."

Scowl. He didn't believe me. "There were a number of impressions in the snow on the path. Are you sure no one else was here Ma'am, someone you may have struggled with?" He glared at me accusingly, wanting to tie up this matter quickly.

I blushed. "Those are my impressions. I slipped and fell and was sprawled out in the snow with all my groceries. There was no one else." I made little circles in the snow with the tip of my boot, trying to avoid his glare. He raised a brow.

"I'm not very co-ordinated," I babbled nervously. He said nothing to put me at ease.

"Well, it looks to me like someone's trying to send you a message, so you must have ticked someone off. Any ideas?" he asked not too politely.

"I don't know anyone in the area, and I'm not aware of anyone that would hate me. Why do you think someone's sending me a message?" I thought of The Ex. No, he'd long since moved on with his life and had been living with another girl for over a year.

"The guy's on display, like it's meant to scare you. Whoever did this wasn't trying to hide him. As a matter of fact, I'd say they wanted him found. I know one thing; he didn't hang himself on that hook." He snorted at his own comment as I recoiled a bit in horror, taking a dislike to him. "You sure he doesn't look familiar?"

"Officer," I said as politely as I could, "I didn't take a close look at his face, but I can guarantee that what I saw did not look familiar." I was not about to look again, and I felt sick to my stomach for the poor man inside my home.

I was advised to spend the night elsewhere while they continued their investigation, and I certainly had no desire to argue. Luckily, my condo was still mine for a few more days, so I trekked back there and called my brother in

Montreal.

"Stephen, don't bother coming tomorrow. There's been a...complication....there may be a day or two delay."

"Hey, Sis, that happens with houses sometimes. It actually works out well for me since we're short a few people at work, so I'll take on some extra shifts and see you in a couple of days." He assumed there was an issue with the closing of the sale and I didn't have the energy to correct him. He'd only blab it to our parents anyway, and I sure didn't feel like dealing with them at this moment.

I ran myself a nice hot bath, poured a stiff drink and settled in for a long soak and a good cry. I was exhausted to the core, both from the events of the day and because of my problematic thyroid that had decided years ago that I was far too energetic. Most days, even though it was supposedly under control with medication, I still struggled with my energy levels and a plethora of other lovely symptoms that really aren't all that lovely.

A couple of days and no clues later, I was given the green light to proceed with my move. They had confiscated the boxes of junk that had been in my office area as possible though unlikely evidence. I had no qualms with it as the boxes had been left there by the previous owners, so it was less garbage for me to deal with.

I was told I could take comfort in knowing that it did not look like the old man had been killed inside my house. For some reason, I did not feel comforted.

Speculation was that he'd been murdered elsewhere by a wound to the head and then dumped at my house, probably because it was vacant. I was informed of this nonchalantly, as though we were discussing the current temperature.

There wasn't much more information, other than that the person appeared to be homeless, but they were working on it. The man had no ID, of course, but they had some leads as to who he might be. But they did not volunteer the information to me.

The crass officer's comment still irked me, both for its lack of compassion and for the warning it entailed. Was someone trying to send me a message for some reason? And if so, why? I was new in this town and knew no one. And, dammit, I was a nice person! Well, except with Hans and his condom.

It was unlikely I'd be in danger, but they'd keep someone on the watch for a few days, just to be sure. This was mumbled half-heartedly, and I didn't feel very assured, and worse, I knew nothing would erase the horrifying discovery from my mind, although loads of wine might help dull the memory over time.

Before moving in my belongings, I took advantage of having one day left at the condo and scrubbed all the walls and floors on both levels of the house and painted some of the walls on the upper level. Once done, I sprayed every nook and cranny in the house with a soothing vanilla-scented room spray to drive away the imagined scent of death and doom and misfortune. I was feeling very macabre and was trying desperately to shake it.

This was going to be my happy place, and I wasn't going to let anything stop me. If someone was trying to scare me off for some reason, then they'd underestimated me. With that as my last thought, I crawled into bed back at the condo, exhausted by all the work I had done.

Two hours later, I was still lying there, staring at the ceiling, at my alarm clock, at the door. I flapped about like a fish out of water, overtired and unable to sleep, the prime condition for worries to swoop in and take over. What if what if what if whirled through my mind, eventually driving me out of the warm cocoon of my bed and sending me pacing back and forth until I again dropped into bed, exhausted, with only a few hours of darkness left.

My brother arrived early the next morning and it didn't take us long to load the moving van. My friend Chloé had also stopped by for a few hours to help, which was greatly appreciated once we were at the new house since bringing some of the furniture up via the narrow outdoor staircase was challenging.

Unfortunately, she surpasses even me when it comes to a lack of co-ordination, so it was no surprise when her help was cut short by an injury. We'd no sooner gotten the couch upstairs when she let out a squawk.

"Damn, my toe! Lift the couch, lift the couch!" she shrieked as we all stared mutely at her feet.

"I hadn't noticed you were wearing those crazy high heeled boots," I couldn't help but comment. I looked at my own practical, warm, flat-heeled boots, then back at hers. We were lucky she'd even made it up the stairs. I had to admit, she looked damn good though.

Barely twenty, she was maybe 5'4" with the heels, with curly, jet black hair and olive colored skin. Chloé was half French, half something else, unfamiliar with the other half of the family as she'd never met her birth father and her mom was tight-lipped about his identity. It was also possible that she didn't know.

Although Chloé normally had a very sunny disposition, she wasn't smiling now and soon hobbled home, leaving Stephen and me to finish up. Luckily all the big pieces had been moved and we could manage with the rest. But I had to admit, her cheerful nature had perked me up.

In all the excitement, I must confess that I had conveniently neglected to mention anything to anyone about the unwelcome welcome package I had found in my office. I thought of it briefly before I quickly pushed it away again. The best way to deal with it was to ignore it.

With the moving van unloaded, we were buried in a sea of boxes. I surveyed the mess around me and sighed in frustration, holding a finger to the pulsating vein that was throbbing above my left eye. Where did I put that dust pan? I had been sweeping up in the living room. It had to be here somewhere. I tore about the room looking for it, doing my best imitation of a Tasmanian devil, my cat

Hummer in hot pursuit.

My brother called out from the kitchen: "Sis, why do you have a dust pan in the fridge?"

Aha! I knew it would turn up. Irked by the smugness in his voice, which clearly indicated that he thought I'd lost my mind, I coolly responded, "Why, where do you keep yours?" I turned and left the room in a huff. Secretly though, I mirrored his reaction. Had I lost my mind? What was I thinking when I bought this building?! Had I made the right decision? I struggled to fight back another moment of panic.

I heard my brother laughing while asking if I was okay and if I minded if he put the dust pan in the small storage pantry off the kitchen. I calmly replied that I was working on my aneurism but would be out shortly. And sure, the storage room would be fine, if he must.

Heaving another sigh, I joined my brother Stephen and poured us both one of my favorite drinks, a Black Raspberry: a healthy slug of raspberry vodka topped with diet Pepsi. I raised a brow, daring my brother to comment. Frankly, I didn't care what time of day it was. To my surprise, he pulled out the two stools from my small kitchen island and gestured for me to sit. We drank in silence for several minutes.

"Do you want me to help you in the living room, or do you want me to finish unpacking the kitchen for you?" he quietly asked as he fidgeted with his goatee. For his safety, I suggested that he remain in the kitchen, out of range of my impending nervous breakdown. With our plan of action clear, we downed the remainder of our drinks, made another, and then resumed the unpacking of boxes.

Other than the odd scraping noises that came from the kitchen, we worked silently for a good forty five minutes before I heard muttering from the other room. "What the freaking fudge? Mali, come here!"

Mali, of course, being me, when people are too lazy to say Amalia. I guess it can get pretty exhausting. I walked slowly to the kitchen, anticipating...what? Bugs? A broken water pipe? A friend mouse for the cat, perhaps? What I found was a lot more interesting...

Stephen stood in front of a door that I had not noticed, perhaps because the former owners had left a wood and glass cabinet behind, which had been secured to what I thought was the wall. Since it was old and rather ratty, and my style was sleek rather than vintage, I'd asked Stephen to get rid of it for me. That explained the odd scraping noises that I had heard as Stephen had removed the unit and slid it out of the spot where it had been.

Both of us stared at the door knob, then at each other, then back to the door knob. All that was missing was some cheesy eighties horror music. Doubting seriously that it would bite, I finally reached out with a tentative hand and turned. It opened with a bit of force, stiff from lack of use.

I grinned at my brother. "After you, oh fearless big brother!" He peered inside cautiously and let out a sigh of relief upon locating a light switch. Miraculously, light flooded a stairwell which, surprisingly, wasn't even old and creepy looking. Nothing to see here, folks, just some dust, I thought to myself. Oh, and one dried up spider, which Hummer promptly sniffed and licked.

We descended slowly, still thinking that something creepy would leap out at us. Reaching the bottom without incident, we turned the knob to the door leading to the lower half of the unit. While the knob turned, the door would not budge. Something was obviously blocking it from the other side. An image of a mop with a coat flooded my mind.

Trudging back up the stairs, then outside and down the stairway, we went around to the front of the building and unlocked the main doors that lead to my future bistro. As I closed the door behind us, a sudden movement, or change of shadow, caught my eye. I squinted into the brightness, eyes roaming over my property until I saw it. A lone, tall figure was slipping into the woods next to my house, the pompom on a winter hat bouncing cheerfully as he or she disappeared from my line of sight.

"Come on, Mali; let's get this over with," Stephen grumbled, disrupting my thoughts. I quickly went to join him and we looked about, trying to determine where the secret stairwell would be situated in relation to the downstairs. I must admit that neither of us was particularly good at getting our bearings. We resorted to inspecting every inch of the walls on the lower unit before finally finding where the door was hidden.

If there was a sign posted saying, "Here's the door," it couldn't have been more obvious, and we grinned sheepishly at each other. In the office area, there was an almost identical, ugly wood and glass shelving unit secured to the wall. Bingo! We made quick work of removing it and voila, the magic door! A quick turn of the knob and it swung into the office with only a slight squeak of protest.

My own secret passage! I made a mental note to check into it with the realtor, in case there was anything of which I should be aware. Maybe there was a reason it was sealed off. As far as I could tell though, it was just a normal stairway offering a way to go up to the residential portion of the house. I could easily slip up or down the stairs without having to set foot outdoors. Which made sense, of course, since this had once, long ago, been a normal house rather than a place of business.

Adventure over, we returned to the unpacking, catching Hummer slyly in the act of sticking his paws into my forgotten drink for a little taste. I should have known better, of course, leaving it someplace where he could reach it. Since he had been a tiny kitten, he had always been sticking his paws into my drinks. When he was first learning to jump, he would leap onto my lap, sticking a paw right into my coffee mug on more than one occasion.

We resumed the unpacking and I caught myself smiling. Having my brother helping me reminded me that although he liked to tease me endlessly, in the end I was always his little sister, and if push came to shove, he'd always be there to help me. Without him there, I surely would have succumbed to the panic. I had no family here in Ottawa, so it was nice having him with me for a couple of days.

By dinner time, we mostly had everything where it belonged and were munching on a nice selection of salamis, cheeses, sliced sour dough baguette and pâté, which were spread out on the coffee table in front of us. Although I prefer wine, we shared another Black Raspberry while sitting on the couch, nibbling. This was actually only my second, I thought to myself, since I'd had to discard the previous, Hummer-infused one.

Exhausted, I looked around at my new home while savoring the smokiness of a slice of Gouda and the slight tang and saltiness of a wedge of Chianti-infused salami.

An older home that had been updated over the years, the house was not big but would be perfect for me. The main floor was dominated by the dining area, which took up more than half of the front portion of the house. The remainder was allocated to the kitchen, a small office and a pantry area. The house was more or less a rectangle with a detached garage to the right of it.

In Ottawa, garages are essential. They keep your car cool in the blistering summer heat and keep it from freezing up in the blustery winter months. It was not a luxury, but a necessity. The only drawback was that it was detached, and there was no doorway linking the garage to the interior of the house. Luckily though, a door lead from the garage to a pathway that meandered to the stairs at the side of the house, which lead up to the door to the upstairs unit.

The upstairs living quarters boasted a good-size kitchen with a modern, but small, island with two leather bar stools, a small pantry area that offered extra storage, a nice size living area, a rather normal size full bathroom, a good size master bedroom (no walk-in closet, however, and my only source of disappointment) and a rather small but functional second bedroom.

It was cozy and smelled of the fresh paint I had applied and a hint of vanilla thanks to the plug-in air fresheners that were now scattered about. The longest wall in my living room area was a soft ocean-blue which contrasted nicely with my mostly espresso-colored furniture and espresso-colored kitchen cabinets. Although I did not have the most modern or top of the line appliances, the white went well with the white marble countertops that the former owners had splurged on. I silently thanked their expensive tastes that ultimately contributed to them having to declare bankruptcy and having to sell their home. I wondered, suddenly, if perhaps the body had anything to do with the former occupants but quickly brushed the thought aside for the time being and returned to admiring my home.

The rest of the walls in the living room and kitchen were a soft mocha-chino color, which almost perfectly matched my couch, armchair and chaise lounge. Cheerful ocean blue and lime-colored throw pillows accented the couch. In front of us was a shiny and cheap, but very retro-chic white Ikea coffee table that I just loved since it contrasted with everything and just "popped", but also drew the eye to the white counters from the kitchen.

With one glance at my home, it was not hard to guess that I'm the type of person who matched the color of a box of Kleenex to the room. I shuddered to myself in mock horror, remembering that not everyone does this.

The mocha walls inspired me to make some coffee. While the coffee was brewing, I put sheets on the spare bed as Stephen would be sleeping over and helping with the bistro the next day.

I prepared two mugs and joined him in the living room. Fidgeting with my spoon, he finally snapped. "You've been stirring that thing forever. Shut up already!" He nudged me with his foot and I smacked him in return. He glared at me, irritated, and I was reminded how different we were. These quick changes of mood defined what growing up with Stephen had been like.

"Sorry. Listen, I have some news that I have to share." I knew I couldn't put it off any longer. He had been fidgeting with his goatee for hours, obviously sensing that something wasn't right.

"You pregnant?" he asked, eyes shining, mood changing again. He knew damn well I'd been single for a long time now so he was just being a wise-ass.

"Only if it's the immaculate conception. Listen, this is pretty serious." I took a deep breath and a sip of coffee at the same time and came up sputtering. I clinked the spoon one more time for good measure. "The day I called you to say there was a complication..." I hedged, then blundered on, "Well, I found a dead man downstairs."

"You finally get a guy in your house and he's dead? Wait till Mom and Dad hear about this," he chortled. I never knew what a chortle actually was, but when he did it, the word suddenly came to mind. I could never understand why, but my brother always took joy in my misfortunes. This, too, defined our relationship.

"Well, I'm not about to tell them, and I'd prefer that you didn't either. There's no sense worrying them since I didn't know the person and this place had been vacant for quite a while. I don't think it had anything to do with me," I said with more emphasis than I felt.

"Alright, I won't say anything. You're right; they'll just worry and then I'll have to listen to it every day, since I live close to them. Just be careful."

I snickered to myself. Since he lived close to my parents, I knew that he had to call them every day since I also had to do that when I still lived in Montreal. I now had them down to weekly calls only.

"I'm beat. Let's call it a night, Steph, we still have lots of work tomorrow. And by the way, thanks again for your help."

"Hey, you're my only sister; of course I'm going to help." With that he gave me an affectionate punch on the arm.

FREAKING FUDGE

IT'S SO FREAKING GOOD!

1 package of plain cream cheese, any brand in the
brick shape
4 and 1/4 cups icing sugar (powdered sugar)
5 large squares (5 ounces) of unsweetened chocolate
squares, melted
2 tablespoons vanilla extract (you can use rum if you
don't have vanilla extract-works just fine)
2 dashes of cinnamon (this is key!)
2 tablespoons cream or milk

Leave cream cheese brick on counter for a couple of hours
prior to mixing ingredients.
Put chocolate and about 2 tablespoons of milk or cream in
a saucepan and melt over low heat, stirring often.

Mix the room temperature cream cheese in a bowl until
smooth and creamy. Add the sugar, one cup at a time and

continue mixing until all added and smooth. It's probably easier to mix with your hands. Next, add melted chocolate and vanilla, and a dash (or two) of cinnamon, mixing well with a mixer until smooth.

If you want to add in nuts or mini marshmallows or raisins or anything, do it now.

Grease a regular size (8 inch or so) square pan and spread mixture as evenly as possible. Store in fridge for a few hours until firm and cut into desired size.

CHAPTER THREE

The next day was another exhausting one, especially since I'd been up a few times during the night, peering out my window, paranoid after having seen someone on my property earlier that day and agitated after not noticing any of the promised police presence.

We cleared out the junk inside the bistro area that the cops hadn't taken, painted some walls a striking red, while leaving other walls either white or, you guessed it, mocha, and on one ten-foot square section we created a large chalkboard. This would be the area where I would have a small bar, the cash register and where we would post our menu.

I set up my office with some furniture that I hadn't been able to fit comfortably in my upstairs living quarters. As the space was small, I didn't need much—I had a comfortable, cheerful yellow wing chair, a small desk, my laptop that I usually kept upstairs, a color printer, a small filing cabinet and one guest chair.

I debated removing the coat hooks that were by the door to erase the memory of what had been there, but in the end my practical side prevailed. The hooks were necessary for my staff to hang their coats. Instead, I hung a colorful and cheery painting of the sun setting over the ocean to brighten the spot.

Luckily, the kitchen area was already equipped with almost everything I would need, otherwise I would not have had enough left in the budget for anything more than a coffee maker and would have had to open a coffee shop instead. Doubting I could compete with Canada's favorite, Tim Horton's, it was unlikely that I would have been very successful in that endeavor.

As this was a bistro and not a restaurant, I wouldn't be doing that much cooking anyway: one or two daily specials, but other than that, my fare would consist of my favorite foods: cheeses, specialty breads, salamis and various appetizers. This was a place to come for a nibble and a drink, gab, listen to music and relax. If you wanted to go out for a fancy meal, you were in the wrong place.

I would, of course, have a nice hearty soup, stew or a casserole available each day to please those who needed just a bit more than munchies— some good stick-to-your-ribs food. But it would be something easy to make as my staff was minimal and consisted of kind friends who already worked other full-time jobs.

Everything was ready for the bistro furniture to arrive. "We'll be there between 9:00 a.m. and 5:00 p.m." I was told. They were not. I was in a tizzy and the aneurism reared its ugly, throbbing head.

What if it didn't arrive for opening night and everyone has to stand? I'd be ruined before I even began. What would I do for a living then? I was ranting and I knew it, but couldn't stop myself.

Stephen wasn't quite sure what to say, so he didn't say anything. I feared he might pluck his goatee right off his face, he was fidgeting so much. Finally, he wisely decided that this would be a good time for a bottle of wine. He rummaged through my boxes and laughed when he found a bottle of white called *Cat's Pee on a Gooseberry Bush*.

Despite its name, it's actually an excellent bottle of Sauvignon Blanc from New Zealand with hints of gooseberry. I liked that they supposedly made a donation to the SPCA, and I was reasonably sure it wouldn't be legal to actually make it with pee.

Exhausted by another hard day peppered with stress, the youthful, citrusy wine zinged right to my brain and I no longer cared about the lack of furniture, lack of sleep and bouncing pompoms in the woods. Bring me more pee.

My brother returned to Montreal early the next morning, and I spent the day planning menus and pacing. Nibbling. Pacing. Swearing. Again, "We'll be there between 9:00 a.m. and 5:00 p.m." I ground my teeth.

I was just about to call them again when I heard a sound behind me. I had been sweeping in the bistro area and whirled around so fast that I almost lost my footing. When I saw him, I froze. Was it possible that he was the tall figure in the woods?

Hans looked just as I remembered him. Extremely tall, expertly coiffed blond hair, clothes more expensive than my own. There was no incriminating hat with a pompom however.

"What are you doing here?" I stammered. "How did you get in?"

"Hey, is that any way to greet an old friend? Relax. I rang the bell at the front and waited forever. Then I went around to the back and the door was unlocked. Come give me a hug."

As he approached, I shrank back. I had not heard from him or seen him in a while, since the time I had insisted that he retrieve the last of his belongings. Our parting had not been amicable.

"How about we skip the hugs and you tell me what you're doing here?" I said less than warmly. "I can't chit-chat too long because of my *condition*, you know; I might need to lie down for a nap," I couldn't resist adding sarcastically.

"I just came to check out your new digs and get the last of my stuff. Quite a place! You must have made a killing on the sale of the condo." He sneered and I took another step back.

"What I sold it for is none of your business. As for the rest of your stuff, I told you when we last spoke that if you didn't come and take everything, I was throwing out the rest, so it's gone. Did you really think I'd *schlep* all your stuff here to my new home and safeguard it for you? I'm not your free storage facility," I practically spat at him in disgust.

He glared at me for a moment. "It's okay; I already know roughly what you sold it for. When it was for sale, I went to see the place and found out the price. I'm pretty sure you didn't accept anything much lower than what you were asking." He sneered again and I could sense where this was heading. He was sniffing around for money!

"You got the car and your RRSPs and six years of my life. I owe you nothing, so you can just get the hell out of here." I marched to the front door, never taking my eyes off him. "Out," I repeated, holding the door wide open.

He stopped right in front of me so that barely a hair separated us and said in a low growl, "You haven't seen the last of me yet."

"Get out!" I yelled. Okay, I pretty much screeched it in my rage. He continued to stand there laughing. To my relief, the delivery truck finally arrived. It was 5:35 p.m. He gave me a final sneer and left while I barely resisted the urge to kick him in the ass.

Shaken and flushed, I was so happy to see the delivery guys that I gave them a jubilant welcome. They dumped everything in the middle of the main room and were gone by 5:49. I fought back tears and looked around at the chaos.

The range of emotions in such a short time span left me drained. Although many things can be said about me, one thing that is never said is that I'm not determined.

With tears streaming down my face, I grunted and groaned, sweated and swore, and managed to push everything around into position except the heavy bar.

I'd done it! Despite the sniffling and panting, I felt a swell of pride. This place actually looked like a bistro!

Yes, it looked cool and trendy. I had some high round tables with high stools, some club chairs with low tables and a couple of long couches with small round tables at either end. The tables were all extremely durable, a glossy red that would not stain and would be easy to wipe down. The rest of the furniture was either dark gray or brown.

Some of it (make that all of it) was bought on credit, one of those "don't pay for a year" plans. I sure hoped that I would have the money to pay for it next year.

One corner of the room had a small stage with a microphone, and my single splurge item, a piano. I do not know how to play, nor do I sing, nor do I have any artistic talent whatsoever, but my best-friend-since-age-twelve, Nicole, had accompanied me to buy the upright grand, and I knew that she would grace my bistro with her soulful musical presence—at least when she wasn't helping me wait tables. In the future I planned to invite local talent to demonstrate their skills.

It was Tuesday, and my grand opening was three days away. I would open my doors to the public for the first time on Friday at 4:00 o'clock. There was still food shopping to be done, as well as posting flyers and delivering as many as possible to local homes in the next few days.

For opening night, my special was going to be a flat fee of fifteen dollars per person, which would include a drink of choice and an assortment of nibbles. Although Nicole was going to help me with food prep and bartending most of the evening, she would be taking the stage every half hour as well. In addition to getting out the flyers, I still had to train Nicole and my other friends, Nora and Chloé, as well as finalize my menu. I made a long to-do list, confirmed with my gals that we'd meet the following afternoon (Chloé declined as she was still nursing her damaged foot), and then dragged myself upstairs for a long, hot soak and a well-deserved glass of wine to erase the image of Hans' smirking face from my mind.

CHAPTER FOUR

My posse arrived the next day as promised. I had been watching out the front window while waiting for them and could have sworn I had seen Hans' car drive by. It was a rare amethyst color so it was not hard to notice. I gave my head a shake, telling myself I was seeing things and being jumpy, but my eyeballs yo-yo'd between staring at the street and looking toward the path that lead into the woods.

Nora was right on time, but Nicole rushed in late, full of apologies and explaining that she'd had a last minute coffee date with someone she had met online. She wouldn't be seeing him again, especially since he'd conveniently forgotten his wallet and she'd had to shell out the cash for the coffee, which, by the way, he had slurped loudly and then left half of it.

Both gals worked full time jobs during the day, and I was lucky that they finished in time to come to 'The Whine' for a 4:00 p.m. start time. For now, my plans were to only be open Fridays through Sundays, so they were both willing to lend a hand and earn a few extra bucks during my start-up. In a few weeks' time, however, I'd also be open on Thursdays, assuming my energy level could take it. I mentally slapped myself. Yes, I would open Thursdays, I told myself with determination.

My future plans might include some wine tasting sessions and special events nights, but that was just a dream at this point. I had a brain bubbling over with many ideas for the future, but I first had to attract customers.

By the time my friends would arrive each day, I would have already cooked the daily hot meal, pre-sliced thick slabs of salamis and cheeses and purchased the fresh bread as well as prepared any other appetizers on the menu for the day.

Once we started taking orders, preparing the plates would be quick, and I was certain the three of us could manage on busy nights, and two of us on quieter ones. If anything, I was afraid no one would come, and that I'd be overstaffed.

My thoughts continued to tumble until Nicole suddenly interrupted her rant about the failed date and my neck hairs stood on end as I heard a shriek. "Amalia! This is so cute!" To say that Nicole is enthusiastic is an understatement. What she lacks in height, she makes up with her voice and exuberance. If you were to hear her before seeing her, you would be expecting a six-foot-tall beast of a woman.

All five feet, three inches of her crushed me into a hug as she jumped up and down with me in her death grip. Try as I might, I could not help envying her absolute cuteness. She was petite, had long, thick, straight blond hair and big green eyes. She worked at the Ottawa School of Dance as a dance instructor, and her shape was enviable. She dressed in a manner that revealed more than I ever would, but I had always been more to the shy side.

Despite her bombshell looks, she was the most down to earth person I knew. She had a sultry, throaty voice, and I was pleased that she would be a regular at my bistro. Like me, she was single; but unlike me, she was a serial online dater. Compared with my two-year empty calendar, she averaged about two or three dates each week.

Nora was another story altogether—an enigma. She, too, was on the vertically challenged side but had an average frame, soft voice and long silver hair. I had worked with her at my previous job for several years, and to this day, I did not know her age, but I think she was roughly fifty-five. She had six grown children and a brood of grandchildren, yet she sparkled with energy.

Her skin was youthful and flawless, with only a couple of little crow's feet crinkling at the edge of her eyes. Like Nicole, she was full of mirth, and I felt blessed to have these two ladies in my life.

Nora had been married for thirty five years to a very lovable man who sometimes just drove her nuts; hence the reason she was here to help. She also owned a hobby farm with five donkeys, a couple of goats, two dogs, a cat and her pride and joy, Chicha the black pot-bellied pig.

Both ladies admired the set-up but stopped short at the sight of the clunky bar in the middle of the room. "This isn't staying here, is it?" Nicole asked, with a perfect Elvis-type sneer, a gesture she'd cultivated since her teens.

"I need your help with this. The delivery was late, so I was on my own. I managed to move everything but the bar. I figured the three of us could manage." I said hopefully.

"Sure, but where's Chloé? It would be easier with four of us." I quickly filled them in about her injured toe as they rolled their eyes, her high-heeled shoe and boot fetish no secret to any of them.

It took a while—after all, I was with two tiny women—but we managed. This time, however, I got hurt in the process, having bashed my knee on the floor when I lost my grip and fell. But there it was, in position near my chalkboard wall, my pain forgotten. It looked magnificent, and I beamed with pride as though I myself had given birth to it.

Finally, we got down to business, which for us meant food. We sat down to the spread I had prepared for them. It was time for taste-testing and familiarizing ourselves with our menu, and I had no doubt that they were both hungry after a full day of work. Naturally, we also had to determine some good wine pairings. How could we sell it if we didn't know about it, right?

As she took a long sip of wine from her second glass (we had enjoyed a glass earlier while waiting for Nicole to arrive), Nora giggled while reading the label on the bottle I had left on the table. "Is this a joke?" she asked, while taking another sip. "It tastes nice, but this is a joke label, right?"

I grinned, unable to conceal my excitement. Voila! My friend had just hit upon one of my bistro's quirks, as had my brother. It was no joke. The wine she was drinking was actually called Ha-Ha.

I specialized, if you can call it that, in finding the quirkiest, funniest named wines that I could get my hands on. The one we had first sampled was called Broke Ass. Which is what I would be if my bistro wasn't a hit.

I don't pretend to be a wine snob. In fact, I don't know or care about all the fancy wine terms like the 'nose' or the 'legs' of the wine. I don't care if it's cheap, and I'm not impressed if it's expensive. What vineyard or country it came from is of no importance to me. If I like what it's called, I buy it. If I like the taste, I buy it again.

"It's no joke, Nora. Let me show you our wine selection." In my excitement, I practically ran over to the bar area where my boxes of wine still sat ready to be placed now that everything else was in position. The girls cackled as they read some of the labels: Bonking Frog. Guilty Men. The Ball Buster. Fat Bastard. Passion. Monogamy. Well Hung. The Velvet Devil.

"Mali, this is fantastic! I love it, it's so original!" said Nora, topping up her glass again. I smiled, liking their reaction. Hopefully it would also be a hit with the customers.

With our glasses in hand, I gave the ladies the rest of the tour, then we went upstairs to tour my living quarters and to discuss menus and Nicole's song selections. Pumped by the positive reaction to the wine names, I was anxious to get started. Once we'd hashed out all the details, we went downstairs to the piano area for Nicole to test the ivories.

I listened in awe, always impressed and surprised when I heard her sing. Having known her for so long, but seldom hearing her sing, I would forget just how talented she was. Her rendition of Diana Krall's "S'wonderful" brought goose bumps to my arms. At the end of the song, she looked over at me and gave me her Elvis sneer to break the suddenly solemn mood.

As my friends parted, I gave each of them a gift bag, explaining that I'd had a couple of T-shirts made for our "uniforms". We had agreed that we'd dress simply and comfortably in black; skirt or pants, whatever they preferred. This would match our color scheme nicely too.

I had gotten a number of custom tees made for each of us. Tunic-style ensured comfort, and the sleeves had a little ruffle, making them cute. Bold red writing stretched across the chest, asking "Some cheese with that Whine?" while another stated "Get some Passion in your life!" (Passion was one of the wines that I carried.) Later, we'd put our heads together and try to come up with something wittier, or hold contests to see which customer could come up with the best lines.

They were already out the door before I remembered that I hadn't told them about the body I'd found. Suddenly feeling watched, I shivered and slammed the door, bolting and triple checking the locks.

THE BEST SPREAD

When my friends and I get together, we often sit around for a couple of hours munching and enjoying a glass or four of wine. Our favorites include:

Hungarian Salami, Thuringer Summer Sausage or a wine infused salami. If you can get it at the deli section, not pre-cut, ask for thick slices- the thickest they can manage, or buy one big hunk and cut thick slabs for yourself.

Garlic and herb goat cheese

Crusty multigrain baguette

Crackers of your choice

Garlic pâté

A spattering of green or purple grapes to unclog our arteries

Arrange all on a platter, provide disposable plates, sit back, nibble, sip, relax and enjoy the company. Why complicate things?

CHAPTER FIVE

Luck was on my side Friday afternoon. For a December in Ottawa, it was surprisingly mild with neither snow, rain nor sleet in the forecast. Decembers in Ottawa have been known to dump a whole winters' worth of snow on you, so this was a rare treat.

Since my handwriting looks like chicken scratches, Nora had written our menu on the giant chalkboard with her tidy, delicate scrawl, while Nicole went about lighting large red and black candles on the tables. I put the finishing touches on my last minute splurge: a glass showcase cabinet which I stocked with a display of various bottles of wine, a nice variety of wine glasses, heavy-duty wine openers, fancy wine stoppers and coasters. All were available for sale should my customers require a last minute gift idea. My gals were now trained on the cash register, and we were all familiar with the menu. It was show time!

In addition to the flyers I had posted and delivered, I had placed an ad in the local paper, announcing the grand opening and our fifteen-dollar special. To my surprise and delight, by Friday most of the tables were already reserved for holiday parties. Even if no other customers showed up, I would still turn a profit on my first night.

Promptly at 4:00 p.m. our first party of eight arrived. We barely had time to seat them and take their order when our next parties of six and four arrived simultaneously. From there, the evening flew with a steady stream incoming and outgoing. And Nicole's jazz sessions were a big hit, if the tip jar on the piano was any indication.

My glass cabinet had also been a success, as crowds would gather around to read the various labels on the wine bottles and share a laugh. Many items were also sold, and I gave myself a mental high-five for my last minute brilliance. My two- year Retail Management course at Dawson College had finally come in handy, my point- of-purchase display the proof.

New to town; I knew no one, but introduced myself to everyone. This was a small town, so it was important to be known and liked if I wanted to thrive. Naturally on the shy side with strangers, I pushed myself out of my comfort zone and did the whole chit-chat thing until I was hoarse and could chat no longer and didn't give a chit. Through it all, I was ever vigilant for bouncing pompoms.

I was surprised to hear tidbits of conversation about the murder and cringed when I remembered that I still hadn't told my friends. I felt a stab of guilt for continuously forgetting that some poor soul had ended up dead in my house.

"I think it's the hoarder-guy who lived close to the train tracks on Robin Road," one woman said in a hushed stage whisper to her friend.

Robin Road was one of two main streets in our town of Robin, and the most popular way of accessing the town. It was also the road on which my bistro was located, as well as the local pizza joint, the post office, the liquor store, the dollar store and the Robin Corner Grocery Store.

Settled in the early nineteenth century as an agriculture

community, train tracks run through the town but trains themselves are now few and far between. When they do pass, they are only a paltry one or two cars long. The town has about six thousand residents and is a mix of farms, old homes, hobby farms such as Nora's, regular homes and more recently, very expensive homes, some multi-million dollars in worth. My clientele this evening was a mixed bag, so characteristic of the neighborhood itself.

With its proximity to the Ottawa River, distant view of the Gatineau Mountains across the river on the Quebec side, and its proximity to downtown Ottawa, the population was slowly increasing as the appeal of country living, while still part of a big city, grew.

I milled about, listening to the tongues wiggling, and hoped I could glean some information. I also hoped that neither Nicole nor Nora heard too much and figured things out before I could clue them in. Don't forget soon became my subconscious mantra.

Other than "We're still investigating, but all we know is that he was a local," I hadn't heard much from the police, nor did I see the police cruisers drive by, although I was assured that they had done so a number of times. I convinced myself that they probably had unmarked cars driving around, and the thought made me feel a bit safer.

Not that I expected the cops to confide in me, of course, or hover over me, but it was unsettling to know that the person that had caused this was still out there. Maybe they were even *in* here. That thought shot a sudden surge of icy panic through my veins. I nervously scanned the crowd with beady eyes.

As we poured wine and delivered platters of food, I jotted down the snippets of conversation that my ears caught. I slowly went to a table next to a group talking and busied myself clearing the items left by the people who had just left. "....I'm sure it was *him*, haven't seen him in days. Sure, he was a bit off, always like that. I grew up with him. Never was friends, though; he stuck to himself. He never said more than hello. That house was his pa's. Always looked the way it does, with all that junk everywhere."

From a table on the other side: "...see him around town every now and then. Always on his own, but sometimes I'd see a car at his house. I was always surprised that anyone would be visiting."

"I saw a woman there a couple of times, opening the gate to the driveway. Always wondered why they'd bother with a gate, as if anyone wanted to steel the crap surrounding that house."

I brought an older couple another glass of wine and noticed that their heated conversation stopped abruptly upon my approach. I flashed a bright smile, and as I moved away, the lady spoke: "You've done very nicely with this place."

Was that a hint of malice in her voice?

"Thank you so much," I replied politely, noting that her companion was openly glaring at me. I faltered. "Is something the matter?"

The man snorted and she shot him a warning glance. "No, everything is fine. We should introduce ourselves. We used to own this place, and Harold wanted to see what you've done with it. I guess it still hurts that we had to sell it, but you have really done a wonderful job." I tried to determine if there was any malice or if she was being genuine.

"I'm flattered that you came, and you're welcome any time. I had a very good base to start with and have you both to thank." I laid on the charm but knew I couldn't let this chance escape, so I followed up quickly with my bombshell. "You wouldn't happen to know anything about the body that was here when I moved in, would you?"

She recoiled as if I'd slapped her, and the man's eyes narrowed. He still hadn't spoken a word.

"My word, that's terrible!" she exclaimed. Although I had no experience grilling people, I decided she truly looked horrified and felt a stab of guilt.

"Are you implying something, Miss?" He finally spoke. It unnerved me how quickly he had jumped to that conclusion, and my guilt disintegrated.

"Of course not. I just thought perhaps you might know something, having been the former owners." I narrowed my eyes at him in return. I could do this, I could be tough. Dammit, I *was* tough. He drained his glass and rose.

"Let's go, Harriet." He was already halfway to the door by the time she even stood. "I'm sorry, dear, he's not usually like this," she apologized, throwing a number of bills onto the table and then rushing to catch up to him.

"Wait!" I caught up to her. "A quick question if I may: Why was the inner stairway blocked off? Is there a problem with it, or did something happen there?" At the risk of sounding rude or desperate, I couldn't let her get away without solving at least one mystery.

"Oh my! Nothing as exciting as that. I wasn't feeling well one evening so I stayed upstairs while Harold and our staff took care of business. While I was taking a bath, a customer wandered upstairs and into my bathroom. I don't know which one of us was more surprised, me or poor Mr. Leonardo. Harold was concerned for my safety after that, so we blocked it off." She smiled wistfully and then dashed off after her husband before I could ask any more questions.

Suppressing a shudder at the naked mental image that she presented, I jotted their names down on my scratch pad, as well as the name of Mr. Leonardo. Possible town pervert?

By 10:00 o'clock p.m., only one party of the original four remained. I couldn't help but sneak another peak at the tall, luscious guy with the sandy hair that flopped just slightly into his eyes. He reminded me of Keith Urban, but with perhaps slightly longer hair and a taller frame. I'm not a fan of country music, but I am a fan of Keith. Oh yes!

Our eyes had skittered past each other a few times

during the couple of hours that he'd been there. This time, mine skittered, but his took a lingering glance. I had heard bits of conversation and knew his name was Matt, but little else.

He was with another guy and two women—the other male and one female obviously an item judging by the game of tonsil hockey they were engaged in. The slender redhead who sat next to Matt had red claws to match and kept pawing at his arm for attention, much like a dog begging for more petting or a scrap of food. I smirked at the thought. She pawed again now, and his gaze switched from mine to hers. Was that a flicker of annoyance?

While he smiled politely, it did not seem to reach his eyes. Or perhaps I was merely wishing. From this distance, I couldn't really tell. Begrudgingly, I couldn't help but notice how beautiful she was.

They rose to leave and Ol' Red wobbled slightly, clutching onto Matt for a helping hand. I smirked again to myself, knowing it was a ploy to try to get close to him. She'd only had one glass of wine, which she'd nursed the entire evening, so it was unlikely that she was that unsteady. I would probably do the same if someone that handsome was in my clutches, so I really couldn't fault her for that.

I called out a cheery adieu and he flashed me a shy smile, cut short as the redhead again tugged on his arm. I locked the doors, gazing briefly at his retreating firm backside before shaking the stars from my eyes and turning away from the door.

We had survived our first night and this Matt was obviously taken, so there was no sense dwelling on him. I can be accused of many things, but man-stealer is not one of them. There was no way that I could compete with that exotic redhead, anyway.

I closed the blinds against prying eyes then balanced the register. We counted our tips. Nicole did especially well, since the piano tip jar was all hers, and well-earned at that! It was a smashing success, with the next couple of weeks guaranteed to be the same if my bookings were any indication.

"Have a seat, ladies", I said wearily. "It's our turn, and we certainly deserve it!" I poured us each a generous glass of Woop Woop Shiraz, amused by my own selection.

When they left the choice up to me, I tended to choose wines that went with my own mood, or from my impressions of people, and I'd had loads of fun doing just that tonight. Ol' Red, for example, had gotten a glass of Bitch. Just cuz... Nothing personal; just me being catty. A group of ladies, out for their monthly escape, each got a glass of Mommy's Time Out. One slightly belligerent gentleman earned himself a glass of Horse's Ass, and I had been tempted to charge him double.

"A toast to a wonderful beginning and great friends! I am indebted to you both for your help. Cheers!" We drank and munched in silence for a few minutes.

I devoured a thin slice of my latest passion, an Asiago cheese, and leaned back to savor the taste, finally relaxing for the first time in days and savoring the moment. This was a fresh Asiago with a smooth texture and interesting after-taste that mingled well with the mild cracker I paired it with. It mingled even better with a glass of red.

Asiago is often compared to Parmesan or Romano as it's very aromatic, in a smelly kind of way. It's best to buy the soft kind that isn't pre-grated or doesn't look too hard. It can be grated on top of pasta like Parmesan, but the taste seems to intensify so I don't like it that way. Just like this was perfect.

When we were finished eating, we discussed the evening, the customers, what seemed to be the most popular items and if we should make any menu changes.I was just opening my mouth to speak when Nicole beat me to the punch. "Hey, did you know some guy got murdered here in Robin?"

I cringed and took a deep breath. "Yes. As a matter of

fact, the body was actually found here, the first day I got the keys to move in." I blurted it out fast. It still seemed surreal.

"No way!" Nora screeched. "Tell us everything." Her eyes shone with excitement or fear, I couldn't decide which.

I recapped the details as quickly as I could. It had been about a week ago now but somehow it seemed as though a lifetime had already passed. They listened in awe.

"So the police officer suggested that someone may have been trying to send me a message, hanging the guy on a hook like that instead of trying to hide the body. They've been driving by regularly (maybe I lied) but stopped in yesterday to say that they wouldn't be continuing the surveillance much longer."

"Well, you be careful Amalia." Nora's cheeks were flushed with what was now clearly excitement and also worry. "Do you suppose it could be personal?"

"I really don't think so," I replied, as I brushed aside the unwanted memory of the Ex and the menace in his voice when we'd last spoken. There's no way he'd want to get blood on his immaculate clothes, I told myself. "Now that the move is finished and the Whine is open, I'll have some time to mull it over. I heard all sorts of rumors flying around tonight, so I took notes. Even the former owners came, and the man seemed pretty jumpy and hostile to me. I don't see that this can involve me in any way, but I thought I'd meet with the real estate agent to ask her a few questions. Maybe it has something to do with them."

"Don't you think the police have done that?" Nicole wondered.

"I really have no clue, because they haven't told me very much. I've been here a few days now and nothing's happened, so I'm almost positive that this place was just random." I said this with more conviction than I felt. "Don't worry; I'll be fine."

We finished our wine and called it a night. I let the gals

out the back door then went upstairs, bringing the days' earnings with me and placing the cash bag in a small safe that I had installed in my closet.

I had decided I would keep only minimal cash in the bistro and the rest upstairs for safe keeping. I would make daily bank deposits but I certainly wouldn't be going anywhere at this time of night since the nearest bank was a good ten minutes' drive away.

I took a quick shower and then snuggled on the couch to watch some mindless shows on the Food Channel, my guilty pleasure and inspiration. I was just starting to come off the adrenaline rush from the evening when I heard scratchy noises coming from the secret passage.

My hackles rose and I froze, holding my breath. Had I forgotten to lock the bistro? Had I forgotten to lock the passage doors? I had installed double locks on the door at the top of the stairway and one at the bottom that locked from my side of the stairwell only, or with a key from the other side, but maybe I was mistaken...maybe I forgot...maybe..."MOW".

MOW? I dashed to the door and opened the deadbolts. I was greeted by two beady eyes, squinting at me accusingly from the dark stairs. A final squint and Hummer marched by, tail twitching in the air. He must have slithered past me when I had come upstairs and, in my exhaustion and pre-occupied state of mind, I hadn't noticed. All was quickly forgiven as he hopped onto the couch, discovering the warm spot I had just vacated. I, of course, did not have the heart to disrupt him, and instead sat in a cold spot, smiling as I watched him clean himself. Yeah, life was good.

CHAPTER SIX

*T*he next day, I reviewed my scribbled notes from the night before and noticed my reminder to myself to call the real estate agent. It was a Saturday, so she'd likely be working. She answered on the third ring.

"Hi Janet, it's Amalia Kis, I bought the restaurant on Robin Road."

"Oh yes, that's right; you must be moved in by now. Listen, I'm hosting an open house right now, but it's over in an hour. How about I stop by and check the place out?" she offered. I accepted.

"That sounds great! Come around the back, Janet, since I'll be in the kitchen." As far as I was concerned, anyone who had been inside my house before I moved in was now a suspect, and I wanted to see if she'd have any reaction to the murder scene.

I was in a sea of chopped vegetables when I heard a knock at the back door. Wiping my hands, I rushed through the office to let Janet inside. I studied her face as she looked around.

"What a cute little office you've set up!" she exclaimed.

"Why don't you hang up your coat and I'll show you

around," I suggested.

She looked around and located the hooks, commenting on the serenity of the painting above it rather than shuddering at a possible memory of hanging a man on the hooks. She looked as cool as a cucumber.

As we passed the doorway to my staircase, she stopped in surprise. "What's this? I don't remember this being here."

"I meant to ask *you* about that. It leads up to the living quarters. It was blocked by a shelving unit at both ends. You didn't know about it?"

"Isn't that interesting? I guess it makes sense, since this was a house at one point."

"There's something else I should ask you," I started hesitantly. Where to begin? I hadn't had much time to think ahead but should have jotted down at least a few questions. "Did you ever meet the people who owned this place before I bought it?"

"Yes, a number of times. They'd been trying to sell it for over a year, and once the sale went through, they paid the mortgage off but declared bankruptcy for all their other remaining debts. They didn't tell me this, of course, but you hear things around here. It's a small town, and word gets around."

"Did they have any enemies?" I prodded.

"Oh, I'm sure they did! I know they owed a lot of money to the local corner store. Their meats are very fresh and they did a lot of their shopping there. The owner let them run a tab for a while, but instead of paying it, they just closed up the restaurant without warning and left town. No doubt they owed money to a lot of people."

"Did many people come to see the house when it was for sale?" I wondered.

"Quite a few. You know, I even thought of buying it myself for a while. You have quite a bit of land and there's all those trails next to you. I had almost decided to go for it when you showed up. I'm not sure what I would have done with all this though, which is why I never acted on the impulse. Now show me around already, I'm dying to see the place!"

An interesting choice of words, I thought, and wondered if she was trying to get a reaction from me.

"Did you hear about the murder?" I blurted out, my nerves taking over.

"Murder? Where?"

"Right here," I said, again observing her closely, "in this house."

She blanched visibly. "You've got to be kidding. Here? I hadn't heard, but I've been working mostly at the opposite end of Ottawa the last couple of weeks and I've had some really late nights. How awful for you. Where was he found?"

I treaded lightly. She had said "he" yet I had not offered that information. Or had I? I wasn't positive and couldn't remember. "In my office—on the coat hooks."

She drew in a sharp breath. "That's hideous. Do they know who he is?" Would I, too, have assumed it was a male?

"Yes, the man lived close by, near the train tracks from what I've heard."

She gasped and started to make her way to the back door, grimacing as she retrieved her coat from the hooks. "You must be getting close to your opening hour, and I've already taken so much of your time. I'll come by another day and you can show me around then." She pumped my hand vigorously then practically bolted out the door before I could even respond.

Why was everyone involved with this house so jumpy?

I spent the next day sleeping and hunting for a local band for New Year's Eve. At times I found myself staring out the front window, squinting intensely at shadows, and I had almost convinced myself that Janet was out there watching me.

By Monday, I was so jumpy that I decided to call

Janet's office to do some snooping.

When the receptionist answered, I blundered forth. "Hello, my name is Amalia and I recently moved into a property that I bought through your real estate office. I'm sorry, I can't remember the name of the agent I dealt with, and I really need to contact her."

"What's your address, please, and I'll see who your agent was." I gave her my address. After some tappity- tap sounds she replied, "Ok, your agent was Janet Renot."

"Oh, yes, that sounds familiar now," I pretended to remember. "She mentioned she had been thinking of buying this house herself. Would you happen to know why?"

"No, I wouldn't have a clue. Is there anything else I can help you with? Do you want to leave a message?"

"Can you tell me, does she work exclusively in the west end?" This was the main reason I had called, remembering that she claimed to have been working at the opposite end of town lately.

"No, none of our agents are exclusive to any particular area, but she actually has most of her properties in the east end. She's one of our few agents that speak French, and the east end tends to be popular with our French clients."

The answer made me exhale the breath that I didn't realize I was holding. So far, that part of her story checked out. She was often at the opposite end of town. A comforting thought entered my mind; even if she was involved in the murder, at least she shouldn't be in my end of town very often and therefore it was unlikely that she was lurking outside. Although it wasn't particularly helpful information, it did succeed in making me feel safer and confirmed that she hadn't been lying.

"You know, now that you told me her name, I found her number right here in my address book. Thank you, I'll call her directly. There's no need to bother with a message." I thanked her quickly and hung up, hoping she wouldn't mention this conversation to Janet.

With our Christmas rush in full swing, the next two weeks flew by. I had placed another call to Janet to invite her back for a visit and to pump her for more information as to why she or someone else may have had an interest in my place. Almost a week had passed with no return call, and I began to grow uneasy. I had no clue what to do next.

I smiled as Nicole described her latest date to us. Not surprisingly, no dates for me, but at least a half dozen for her. I wasn't sure if I secretly envied her, or if I was concerned with how many people she randomly met.

"So, last night, I met this guy for dinner instead of just for coffee. We'd been chatting for a while and really seemed to hit it off, so I figured what the heck, right? I'll break my coffee only rule. So get this, I arrive and he's already on his second drink, but worst of all, he's missing a bunch of teeth. Total turn off right away, but I had to last through dinner and I'm thinking to myself, Nicole, this is why you usually only meet guys for coffee, right? Then he tells me he has a kid with an ex, and because he hasn't paid his child support, his license was taken away and would I mind driving him home afterward! Anyway, so no teeth, no license, deadbeat parent and all this before I even had a chance to order food. I excused myself to go to the bathroom and just walked out without looking back. Can someone tell me what holes these guys crawl out from? And why do they zero in on me?" Her tirade ended with a wail.

"You know, maybe you should take a break from that online stuff. You haven't met anyone there that you've actually stuck with for more than a date or two. Don't you worry that one of them might try to go after you or something?" My concern grew when she suddenly looked uneasy.

"Maybe you're right. Now, don't panic, but he did come after me once he figured out that I was trying to bail. He almost caught up to me before I made it to my car, and I got pretty nervous. I managed to race off just in time with my horn blaring to attract attention in case he tried to jump on my car or something. If I don't meet anyone soon, I'll give it a break for a while, I promise. Geez, I'll have so much spare time that I can help you once you open on Thursdays," she said as she walked to the front door to unlock it, but not before I noticed her anxiously peer outside.

"Are you expecting your ex?" she asked hesitantly. My skin instantly puckered in response. "Because I swear that's him sitting out there in his car." Nicole had met him many times over the six years we'd dated and had never really warmed up to him.

I marched over and looked out. Sure enough, there he was, sitting in his car and looking our way. I opened the door and glared at him, pointing my finger and shouting, "Go!" I could see him laughing and giving me a wave with his middle finger as he drove away.

"What's that all about?" Nicole and Nora asked in stereo.

"I'm not really sure, but he showed up here the other day. Right now, he's just trying to intimidate me...I think." Unfortunately, it was working. I noticed my hands trembling slightly. It was not like Hans to put an effort into anything other than his own looks, and considering he didn't live anywhere near this area, it definitely had me stumped. I didn't have time to dwell on it much longer though; I had work to do.

Within half an hour, the customers started to arrive. I was pleased when I recognized a number of repeaters. As always, the evening flew by.

I had placed another ad in the local flyer, advertising our New Year's Eve special. Knowing this was the best time of the year for restaurants, I had to make as much money as possible before the quieter months settled in.

A couple of days later, Nicole and I were finishing the New Year's Eve decorations when I overheard her taking another call for a reservation. "Four for Matt? And your telephone number, please..." My ears twitched and my stomach did a little triple Lutz when I heard her say the name, but I quickly ignored it. Anyway, it was unlikely that it was the long haired, rugged Matt from opening night. And plus, he'd likely have 'The Red Claw' with him. I mentally ejected him from my mind and returned to the task at hand.

With Christmas now over, I was giving the glass display cabinet a makeover. I had decided on a New Year's/winter theme with scarves, hats, streamers and mittens decorating a fresh display of whimsical wine bottles: Live, Laugh, Love, Bad Habit, Live-a-Little, Daddy's Happy Juice and when in doubt, Wine is the Answer—all for sale, of course.

Once that was done, I started on preparations for the next day while Nicole continued with the decorations. As today was Tuesday, we weren't open, so we had time to prepare what we could ahead of tomorrow's party. It would likely be our busiest day, since the area only boasted two places where one could go out and party—one advantage of operating in a small town.

My hot dish would be a traditional tourtière: a blend of three ground meats in a flaky puff pastry, my own creation. I was not a fan of traditional pie crust, and I was not very talented with a rolling pin, so I couldn't make my crust from scratch. Forced to find a tasty alternative, I had discovered the world of puff pastry, which made a wonderful topping for my meat pies.

I prepared the meat filling and would spoon it into the puff pastry the next day so that the work on party day would be minimal. I would also be making a Hungarian Goulash, so I pre-chopped everything in advance and stored the ingredients in containers so all that was left to do was throw everything into giant pots the next day.

I couldn't wait to see my bistro filled with customers.

FLAKEY BEEF PUFF PIE

This is easier than a tourtière.

> 1 lb (450g or so) extra lean ground beef (or a mix of ground beef, pork and veal)
> 1/2 large chopped Spanish (red) onion
> 1 cup good quality tomato sauce (whatever kind you like)
> 1 cup shredded cheese of choice
> 1 cup chopped veggies of choice (celery, green or red peppers, mushrooms or a mix)
> Salt, pepper to taste
> 1 teaspoon chili powder
> 1 teaspoon garlic powder
> 1 teaspoon of sugar, if sauce is slightly bitter
> 1 ready to use package of puff pastry

Brown meat then strain off fat. Add veggies, if using any, and sauté, then add rest of ingredients except for puff pastry. Simmer 20 minutes to blend. You can do it for less, but I like to simmer it longer.

Use baking dish of choice. I usually use a glass pie-sized dish. Spray it lightly with cooking spray, then line bottom with puff pastry. Spoon mixture onto pasty, then top with another layer of puff pastry (use according to package directions). Bake 20 minutes at 350 F. Let stand a few minutes before serving.

This is great with a green salad. Or fries. Or both if you're feeling guilty about eating fries. It can be made ahead and frozen; just thaw overnight in fridge before baking.

CHAPTER SEVEN

The next day was filled with the buzz and electricity that could only be associated with an upcoming New Year's Eve party. Everything was decorated beautifully, and to my relief we were booked solid. The place was quickly filling up and I had succeeded in hiring a local band to play dance- style music. I would need both Nicole and Nora for waiting tables tonight, so Nicole would only hit the stage after midnight, once we needed people to start winding down.

Although I'd been counting on her, Chloé still wasn't able to help, claiming that her foot throbbed in her heels if she was on her feet for long. When I recommended wearing flats, I was greeted with a gasp and a one word response: "Never!"

It was almost 11:00 p.m. before I noticed—or rather, felt—HIM. Feeling the little hairs rising on my neck, I turned and stared into those astonishing green eyes. He wasn't touching me, of course, just looking at me, and quite frankly, he wasn't even anywhere close to me. I felt a flush begin in my toes and quickly work its way up to my bangs. Dang, it was hot in here!

I started to smile, and then stopped abruptly when I noticed a petite woman with long black hair clinging to him. This wasn't the redhead. My secret crush apparently was a player. For some reason, this disturbed me, even though just a moment ago I hadn't hesitated to consider flirting with him. With some effort, I pasted the smile back in place and marched over before Nora or Nicole intercepted.

"Happy New Year everyone! Let me show you to a table. Thank you for coming again; you were here once before, I believe?" I realized I was rambling but couldn't stop myself and I felt myself flush furiously so I continued, barely giving them a chance to settle down. "What would you like to drink?"

Matt hesitated before speaking: "Yes, we were here before. I had a great wine that night, but I can't remember what it was. What do you recommend?" he asked with a glint in his eye and with a voice that seemed to stroke my skin gently. Well, it stroked something, anyway.

Normally I love this question, but I was not able to tell him what I had in mind. How about a nice red Well Hung? I mentally snorted to myself. Or how about Guilty Men? Or Pro-Mis-Q-ous? Instead, I said sweetly, "How about a little Monogamy?" He blinked in surprise before murmuring, "Yes...yes, that sounds absolutely perfect." I later brought him a second, possibly putting it down in front of him a little too brusquely, and his eyes snapped up to bore into mine. I blushed, realizing I was acting like a jealous girlfriend when really I was...well, I was just simply his server. His and his new girlfriend's server...

I slunk away to attend to the surrounding tables. One in particular left me somewhat uneasy. The trio of men seemed nice enough, but unlike the other party goers, I didn't sense a happy aura around them. I could feel their eyes on my every move, watching me intensely. I almost ran from their table each time in my haste to escape their scrutiny, but my curiosity started to kick in. I wasn't that stunning to be the subject of such close scrutiny, especially from three men at once, so there must have been another reason. I forced a smile and tried to loosen them up a little.

"I don't recall seeing you gentlemen here before. Are you from the area?"

They exchanged an uneasy glance. "Uh, no," one of them stammered. "We just heard about the place and thought we'd check it out." The other two nodded mutely.

"Do you know anyone from around here?" I continued casually. I had only placed an ad in the local paper and I doubted that word of my small bistro had made its way too far.

"Nope, can't say we do," he replied rather brusquely, the other two now shaking their heads in unison like marionette puppets. There was nothing distinguishable about any of them, all three with an average build, with regular brown hair, plain haircuts and plain clothes. As I took a closer look, I noticed all three were in jeans with black t-shirts. I could smell a hint of cigarette smoke clinging to the air, and my nose twitched as I was allergic to cigarette smoke.

"Well, I'm flattered that you've heard of my bistro, and thank you for coming to check it out. Are you here because of the murder?" I was as surprised as they were that it had jumped out of my mouth.

The spokesman responded again. "We did hear something about that, now that you mention it. Was it a friend of yours?" His reply was innocent enough and I felt bad for having blurted it out.

I shook my head. "No, I didn't know the man. This place had been empty for a while, so I guess that's why this place was chosen. Well, have a good time gentlemen." I smiled again then moved on, sensing I was making them uncomfortable and feeling silly for having brought up the murder. Maybe they were just painfully shy. Heck, maybe I was attractive enough to have three men swooning over me and watching my every move. It must be the caramel hair.

I signalled for Nora and whispered for her to take over the table for the rest of the night, explaining quickly that they kept watching me and it was making me nervous.

At midnight, I couldn't help but sneak a peek at Matt's table. While the couple he was with inspected the inside of each other's throats with their tongues for several minutes, he and the dark-haired beauty exchanged a quick chaste kiss on the lips that barely lasted a nanosecond. Much to my unabashed joy, I might add. Then, they sat uncomfortably while they avoided looking at the love birds, or at each other. He caught me staring and I quickly turned, unable to hide my smirk or my blush despite the dark and cozy atmosphere.

I looked around wistfully, watching all the happy couples sharing New Year's kisses. I sighed softly. I was okay with being single but was also aware of how alone I was at times like this. Suddenly I felt an arm around my shoulders, and I jumped in surprise. Nora let out a squawk in return.

"Geez, you're jumpy! Relax, I was just giving you a little hug; you looked really sad."

"Nora, I'm so sorry. I'm so selfish. It never occurred to me that you might like to be home with your husband tonight."

"I've been with him for over three decades. We don't even kiss anymore," she replied with a smile on her face. "Tell me, did you and Hans kiss much after five or six years together?"

I had to think about that for a moment. "I guess you're right. The passion does go away after a while." I looked over at Matt and couldn't picture the passion ever fading. He caught me looking again and arched a brow in my direction before someone walked by, blocking my view. When I could see him again, his date was whispering into his ear, so I turned away and returned to my work. No doubt she was suggesting fun and games back at her place.

Before I knew it, we were wrapping things up and settling bills. With a sigh on my lips and a tingle in my loins, I approached Matt's table with the bill. The two men divvied things in half, and when I gave them their change, Matt pressed a number of bills into my hand, grazing my fingers with an electric jolt that I couldn't deny.

"Thank you for a wonderful evening; it's very lovely here. Beautiful ambiance". Again, the stroking-of-the-skin voice. I did a Hummer-like blink in return but could think of nothing crafty to say other than muttering "Uh, thank you. Happy New Year!" And with that, they were gone.

Yep, I had apparently forgotten how to flirt. But then again, he seemed to have his share of admirers, so there was no point anyway. I certainly didn't want to be Miss Wednesday night. Or did I? Would a fling be so bad? As I was cramming the tip into my pocket, something caught my eye. I blinked as I read the name 'Matt' along with a phone number. That's all there was. No cryptic message. No declaration of lust. No apology that he was a philandering weasel. Never the less, my fingers tingled. Miss Wednesday night? Could I do that, with no strings attached?

Nora appeared at my elbow. "Hey, was that Mr. Smoking Hot? I wish I would have seen him sooner; maybe I would have given him a New Year's smooch!" With that she cackled and moved on. I knew full well she'd do no such thing, but the image put a smile on my lips.

I was just settling the bill for another table when one of the men grabbed my hand. "Hey, Sweetie, nice place you got here. I was over at the pizza joint the other day and let me tell you, Ol' Leo ain't happy about you opening this place." The booze from his breath made my eyes smart. I was sure my contact lenses were melting.

Shivers ran up my spine at his words, and I wondered if Leo could be Harriet's Mr. Leonardo who had walked in on her in the bath. "Oh, my goodness, I'm so sorry to hear that. I've made sure that our menu's not similar to his so that I wouldn't take business away from him," I assured the gentleman. And I had too, having received his menu in my mail and making sure I didn't serve the same food that he did. Of course, there was no danger there: he specialized in pizza, and again, I couldn't roll dough to save my life; I had no doubt that if I were to try to twirl it above my head, I would end up wearing it.

"Yeah, well, tell that to Leonardo. If I were you, I'd go over with a peace offering and get on his good side. I'd sure hate to see him run you out of business." He winked, paid his bill and sauntered off. Was that some sort of threat? Had Mr. Leo sent him over here to scare me or spy on me? Had he been watching me this evening? I suddenly remembered the other three men and glanced over at their table, but they'd already left. Were they sent here by Ol' Leo? That might explain why they had been watching me so intently.

It was late; we'd been open well past our usual hour. Throughout the evening, I had periodically snuck upstairs to put the cash into my safe, paranoid with so much money lying around in the bistro. And perhaps I refreshed my makeup and put on a fresh spritz of perfume, but I'm not admitting anything.

I put the last of the cash into a deposit bag and left it on my desk in the small office as I let Nicole and Nora out the back door, closing it quickly as a blast of cold air came rushing inside. It was a blustery minus 28 Celsius. Happy New Year!

I went about doing a final inspection of the bistro area and closed the blinds. Making my way back to the office, I froze and whirled suddenly, thinking I had seen a shadow in one of the windows. Again, I blinked, clearing my bleary eyes. Nothing. The blinds were closed, of course; I had just done that. Feeling more than just a bit paranoid, I walked back to the front window and peered out from a corner.

Maybe it was from being single for a while now, or

from not having any immediate neighbors, but I liked to make sure all was secure. There was nothing of course, but I still felt a bit spooked, as if I was being watched. Call it something in my latent gypsy blood, but I just had the heebie-jeebies. I glared, imagining Hans out there somewhere, still laughing at me. No, he wouldn't be out in this cold weather—his hair might freeze.

Turning out the last light, I beat a hasty retreat upstairs and quickly bolted the two locks once I was at the top. Safe. I looked over at my guard cat, waiting patiently for me in the kitchen. Yes, blinking. We were very much alike.

Of course, in all the excitement I had forgotten to give him his evening treat. I opened a can while he danced about my legs. All was forgiven. I proceeded with a long hot shower and was just nestling down in bed when I bolted upright. I had forgotten the money bag on my desk.

I stuck a foot out and placed it on the floor. Cold. Sighing, I brought the foot back in bed. The money would be fine—most of it was already in my safe after all. It was too cold to worry about it.

I was dreaming of Matt. This time he was with a taller woman with caramel-colored hair. In this dream, my hair was shinier and longer than it was in real life. I had a hand firmly clamped on his arm, my red claws gleaming under the lights, while he looked over my shoulder. "Get out!" he said sharply. I looked up at him, tears in my eyes. "But it's my bistro, why should I get out? Don't you love me?" I wailed like a damsel in distress, my feelings hurt.

He continued to look over my shoulder and issued a throaty growl. As I looked on in surprise, his eyes glowed, and the growl became deeper as he drew his lips back and bared his teeth. He jumped onto my stomach, and then I bolted awake. Hummer was growling and had used my stomach as a springboard before running out of my room.

As I listened I broke out in a cold sweat, imagining that I could hear footsteps. My blood was pounding in my ears. I slunk out of bed, careful not to make any noise. It was unlikely that anyone could break into my living quarters, but you never know. I reached under my bed for the bat that I kept there.

I found Hummer sitting by the door to the secret passage, ears flat on his head. The odd grrrr still escaped him every few seconds. I sat next to him, listening, my own teeth bared. We were motionless for an eternity but I heard nothing. When I returned to bed, he settled in for the long haul, keeping watch by the door. I debated going downstairs but chickened out half a dozen times before falling into a fitful sleep.

The next morning, I found Hummer still by the door. I was a bit creeped out until, seeing me awake, he gave me a couple of barks—I swear, the cat barked—before wrapping himself around my legs. I praised him, of course, for his prowess as a guard cat and thanked him for keeping me safe. "Who's my good boy? You're so handsome," I complimented, as his tail twitched in response.

As the last of the coffee gurgled into the pot, I decided to dash downstairs for some Baileys. I would have a special New Year's Day treat and return to bed to watch TV for a while, ringing in the New Year with some much needed rest and relaxation after the last few busy and profitable weeks.

I turned on the passage light but nothing happened. I flicked the switch a few times. Nothing. Either the bulb was burnt, or I had left the bottom switch in the middle position and therefore it wouldn't work from the top.

I grabbed my trusty cell phone and engaged the flashlight app for some lighting. I dashed downstairs, with visions of Baileys dancing in my head, and stumbled at the bottom as my foot struck something. Losing my balance, I fell face first against the door, which then swung outward. I almost fell into my office.

I turned quickly, in panic, my thoughts now swirling. My door was unlocked. There was a lump on the landing at the bottom step. I remembered bolting the locks upstairs. And the lump was large. But admittedly, I did not recall locking the bottom door.

I aimed the light at the lump and it let out a sinister growl. I recoiled and caught a glint of eyeballs. Hummer had followed me and it was he that growled, unhappy with the obstruction in his path. The lump, however, was mute and motionless. It was also covered in blood.

What do you think, this is a recipe book? Keep moving. This hardly seems like the time for a snack, someone else just got killed!

CHAPTER EIGHT

*T*he cops arrived within twenty minutes. I quickly called Nicole, who lived fairly close, and asked if she'd be able to zip over as there had been a break-in and another body.

I answered a bevy of questions a number of times to a number of people. No doubt the different cops wanted to make sure my story matched each time. The man was dead, of course, but other than being able to confirm that he looked like someone who may have been in my bistro the night before, there was little else I could say. He did look vaguely familiar, in his jeans and black top, but I had to admit that I had spent a good bit of the evening admiring Matt.

Did I know him? No. Was I dating? No. When was the last time I dated? I answered with a glare, not wanting to disclose that it had been two years. Did I have enemies? Well, apparently the pizza guy, my ex, and one of the former owners disliked me. Could anyone vouch for the events of the evening? I confirmed that one of my co-workers should be here shortly, and any of my customers could likely vouch for me since the place had been packed. They advised me that I could return upstairs but that I was not to touch anything on the main floor or the stairway until they cleared the scene.

As New Year's Day was a national holiday, I would not be open. I worried if the following night, a Friday, would be affected. When I asked, Cop One merely shrugged and scowled. I then asked if I could go get my bottle of Baileys. He scowled deeper, which I assumed meant no.

I returned to my coffee, sans Baileys, but with extra cream and sugar. I had only made enough for one cup but quickly made a full pot, some flaked ham roll-ups and a platter of cheese. I added some double cream Brie, a few round slices of Provolone, the decadent fresh Asiago and some cheese curds. By now it was nearly noon and I was starving, the adrenaline rush wearing off and the shock settling in a bit.

I had a quick bite, half-heartedly fixed my hair and slapped on some make-up (I had to admit that Cop Two was kind of cute) and then brought the coffee and food down, using the outside stairway and knocking on the back door, not wishing to disrupt any possible prints or evidence. I was an avid reader of murder books so I fancied that I knew a thing or two about the basics.

Cop Two also scowled when he saw me at the door. Perhaps it was a pre-requisite? But it quickly turned into a half-smile as he saw me bearing gifts. He allowed me into my office area where I put everything on the desk. I felt something in my gypsy blood tingle. Cop Two the cause? I glanced more closely at him. No, not my type; he was rather on the doughy side. But something was not quite right. A prickly feeling. Something out of place? Skin rash? I have very sensitive skin, so maybe an allergic reaction...hives from the stress perhaps...no...wait...

My money bag was gone!

"I have more to add to what I said earlier," I told Cop Two, flustered. Officer Sean, I read on his badge. "I left a bag of money on my desk last night, and just now noticed that it's gone". My stomach roiled, not just from the loss of the money but from the sudden sense of violation I felt. The murder itself was committed against someone else, but this theft was against me.

"Gone, eh? And you didn't think of this earlier? Why?"

"I usually bring the money up to my safe so I hadn't remembered that I'd forgotten some on my desk last night when I'd gotten spooked." I blurted this out, sounding like a kid in first grade with poor grammar.

He raised a brow and scowled.

With my face beet red, I raced on. "I thought I'd seen something in the window, but there really was nothing. But I still felt spooked, probably just because it was late and I was tired, so I bolted upstairs. Afterwards, I was just too tired to come back down." I did not add that Hummer practically insisted that I stay in the warm bed with him.

"I suppose you're going to tell me there was thousands of dollars in there, so there's a record for insurance purposes?" His voice dripped with scorn as his scowl deepened.

"No, as a matter of fact, there was maybe only around two hundred dollars, if that. I'd brought most of the cash upstairs during the evening. Nothing worth making a claim for..." I smiled a sweet smile. Hey, I'm the good guy, I felt like saying. Look at me, I'm sweet and cute! I have make-up on. For gosh sake, I have caramel-colored hair.

That got me a brow lift and a chicken scratch on his note pad, as though he had read my thoughts. "Ok, we'll be checking outside as well to see if there's any sign of someone lurking around, or any nose prints on your window. You go on back upstairs," he snapped at me as he turned and walked to the front of the bistro. I wasn't sure if I should salute, but I was about to follow orders when Nicole arrived.

I talked fast to fill her in. "I thought I saw something last night, but I didn't, and then I thought I heard something, but I wasn't sure and then I came down here this morning and tripped over something. A man is dead on my stairs, and some of the money from last night is missing!" Her eyes widened in shock but before she could ask any questions, Sean returned. Scowling. Furiously.

"I thought I told you to go upstairs," he started, then suddenly, a smile, wide and bright as the sun itself. "Is this your witness?" he asked sweet as pie, his smile widening until I could practically see his wisdom teeth. I introduced Nicole and the smiled widened even further. He looked like a Cheshire cat. To me, however, the usual scowl. "You may go back upstairs while I speak to Nicole". He purred her name.

Turning back to Nicole, he smiled again as he began the questions. I sighed and slunk back upstairs with my tail between my legs. Nicole the beauty strikes again!

Hummer and I had another coffee to cheer ourselves up since we weren't really sure what else to do. He likes his with extra sugar. I had placed my mug on the coffee table while I busied myself with a to-do list, and he took advantage of this distraction and stuck his paw in my cup. He was just licking it clean and looking very proud of himself when I noticed. The rest went down the drain since I was pretty sure too much coffee wasn't good for cats. He blinked his disagreement.

Nicole came up to join me after a short time. She was not scowling. I rolled my eyes in frustration, pretty certain that she had a date lined up with the officer.

"I can't believe this happened!" she exclaimed, her cheeks flushed. "I'm not sure if this will be good for business or really bad—people love gossip and can be pretty macabre, so it could go either way. The first one didn't seem to affect business. Do you think it's connected to the other murder?"

I, too, wondered if they were connected but I had tried to push those thoughts aside. I was hoping for the latter, of course, that curiosity would help to draw a crowd again. But what if it didn't? And what kind of person did that make me, hoping to benefit from this? It was bad enough that another body had been found in my bistro and that I had found both, the memory forever imbedded in my brain. But yet, I had to be realistic. What if everyone was scared away and I lost everything? I had to come up with a plan, even at the risk of offending others.

Having some time on my hands while I waited around, I'd jotted down some ideas. I struggled silently before answering Nicole. I didn't want to be insensitive however I did have a new business to run and a home at stake too.

"I'm starting to think that it can't be a coincidence," I faltered. It sounded much different when said out loud than it had in my head. I shivered before continuing. "And maybe that cop had been right when he said that maybe someone was trying to send me a message." I faltered again. "So, I think my best plan of action is not to let it show that it's scaring me, and I think I have a plan to do just that. Remember that year when we went to a murder mystery dinner?" I looked up at her, anxious to see her reaction, to see if she'd be horrified by my idea and find me repulsive.

"Yes! That would be perfect; you're brilliant!" I sighed in relief then showed her the notes I'd doodled while waiting for her.

"So, I did some research and found some appropriately named wines we could showcase, and I'm going to call the number of the restaurant that had the murder mystery dinner in downtown Ottawa. Perhaps I could hire their crew, or they could make recommendations." I sounded more certain of myself than I really felt, but I knew I had to figure out a way to turn this unfortunate event around. I had to. I had just over one month of severance pay left and then no income other than what the bistro brought in.

I looked at my list. "Nic, want to come downtown with me tomorrow for some shopping?" I had a list of wines that weren't currently in my stock that would be perfect: the ever well worded WTF. Even better, a bottle of Ooops and a Holy Cow, accompanied by a chaser of The

Accomplice and Eat, Drink and be Scary. I wrote down one more that summed things up nicely. Gross. In red, of course. Poor taste, perhaps, since my stairs still had splatters of blood. My smile faltered at the memory.

"Um, sure, I'm off for a few days since there's no dance classes during the Christmas break but...uh...how about 1:00 p.m. instead?" Nicole suggested, looking sheepish. "I kind of have brunch plans," she finally admitted.

A date with Officer Sean, no doubt. I didn't ask; didn't want to know. I mentally tucked my tail between my legs again. Where Nicole excelled at dating, I excelled at... I'd think of something. I'm pretty sure that drinking wine is a talent.

By noon the next day I had the all clear. They were satisfied that they had gathered all possible evidence. There were many prints, no doubt all of them ours. Footprints were out of the question as there were simply too many. The back entrance had been used by me, Nicole, Nora and the local band and the front had been used by my clientele.

Other than a large number of dents in the skull of the victim, there really didn't appear to be any evidence, or so I gathered. The murder weapon, however, was easy to determine and I suspected this was why I was able to re-open so soon. It was rather obvious really: the man had been killed by having his head bashed repeatedly onto the stairs on which he lay. I wondered if the first victim had died the same way but did not dare ask. In any case, they had assured me at the time that the first man had not been killed on my premises.

Although I'm not particularly squeamish, I do have a gag reflex, so I was happy to see that the stairs had been professionally cleaned for me. I could smell something piney as I went down the stairs and walked about for a look.

Although the stairs were clean, the rest of the place was another matter. I would have to mop the floor since there were wet footprints everywhere, and wipe everything down where there appeared to be fingerprint dust. I did that quickly, then paused briefly next to the reservation book as Matt's name and phone number caught my eye. I smiled. Although the bill with his number on it had been in the stolen money bag, I still had his number in my book. I'd have to think about it. I hurried out the door to pick up Nicole for our downtown rendezvous before I did anything I'd later regret.

I raced over and was not surprised that I was being followed. I fought back the sudden panic with logic. Of course, since the murder happened at my bistro, I would be a suspect, and since there were now two murders, they'd definitely be more interested in me than ever. On a good note, if the cops were following me, then I'd be safe.

"I thought you'd never get here," Nicole said as she leaped into the car, rubbing her hands together. Once again, it was a balmy twenty below zero, Celsius. Being a transplant from Montreal, I was still always surprised how much colder and snowier Ottawa was compared to its neighbor that was only two hours away. Of course, Ottawa is known as one of the snowiest capitals in the world. Lucky us!

I engaged the GPS and continued to downtown Ottawa, not mentioning the cops to Nicole, knowing she'd be paranoid. I did not go downtown often, but often enough to know that I simply had to depend on my GPS. Like other big cities, there were many one way streets, construction sites, and streets that changed names three or four times from one end to the other. Having lived downtown for a while had been of no help. At the time, I either walked everywhere or took a bus. Downtown Ottawa via car is very different. And, well, maybe my sense of direction just isn't the best.

I parked in an above ground parking lot on Clarence Street, in the heart of the Byward Market. Here we'd be close to everything and, due to the extreme cold, we wouldn't be dawdling as we do in the summertime during the various festivals.

Having moved here only two years earlier from the Toronto area, Nicole loved the Byward Market, as I'm sure all locals and tourists do. Ottawa has a business district in one section, with all the taller buildings in one area. This section includes Spark Street, a very quaint cobbled street that was often closed to traffic while it hosted special outdoor events such as the summer busker festival.

Next, we have the section with the parliament buildings, the infamous Chateau Laurier, the National Arts Centre, and the National Gallery of Canada, an art museum once famous for making a big to-do about a painting that consisted of two colors. The Voice of Fire cost the city 1.8 million dollars and was two navy blue stripes with a red stripe in the middle. I recalled having done a similar piece in kindergarten. I, however, did not get 1.8 million dollars for my efforts.

Not far from the art museum, we have our Byward Market, a charming area with a plethora of restaurants, many that offer outdoor dining during the warmer months, cafés, outdoor markets, deli's and a representation of many different cultures and languages. The majority of the action took place on about a half-dozen streets that hosted many outdoor festivals in the summer. The only festival that I knew of in the winter months was Winterlude, when ice sculptures and skating on the Rideau Canal while munching on a Beaver Tail pastry were the Ottawa thing to do.

Today, however, was a day to just get what we needed and then get back home. We went first to the Byward Market Square and then to York Street to visit two of my favorite deli's.

Although I get many of my products direct from suppliers, at a much better price, nothing beats shopping in person in these local delis. It reminded me of my youth when my parents would take me to similar deli's in the

Montreal area. Not all of my childhood memories are bad. Growing up Hungarian was at times difficult, but I can appreciate it now that I'm older and speak three languages. I do, however, blame my addiction to salami on my upbringing and can almost visualize my arteries protesting in horror each time I have some. My father's heart attack a number of years ago was proof that what we ate wasn't exactly healthy.

We stocked up on some items that had our mouths watering: Hungarian kolbasz, which is a smoked Hungarian sausage, some Emmantel cheese, garlic and herb Havarti. I was drooling. As we were rushing back outside into the cold, we collided with a man just outside the door who looked as though he was debating on whether or not to go inside. As he glared, we apologized and then hurried off, not sure if he was one of the many homeless people that also frequent this area. In the back of my mind, I wondered idly if he was one of the cops that were following me.

We made our way toward the liquor store on Rideau Street that carried the wines I was looking for and then stopped at the Rideau Centre for a bite to eat at the mall's food court. Finally, it was time to hurry back to the bistro.

Nicole was the first to see him and nudged me with her elbow. "Look, it's the guy we ran into!" She stopped, pretending to tighten the laces on her boots and indicated slightly with a slow chin cock. I casually turned my head and saw him across the street, walking slowly and about ten paces behind us.

Before I could commit any details of his appearance to memory, he walked into a store. As we started to move on, I felt myself shiver. "Did you notice that although he went into the store, he seems to be standing near the door?" I quietly asked Nicole. We were now convinced he was following us and I had to admit, he didn't look like a cop to me.

We walked about twenty feet before she dared to steal

a peek behind us. "Well, at least this time he's a bit further behind". Her voice was tight.

We looked at each other, with wide eyes. What the heck? The homeless were known to be bold at times (I once had one man ask me if I could spare $100), but truth be told, he didn't look homeless. A bit on the scruffy side with some stubble, but otherwise he was wearing a business suit underneath his heavy winter coat.

We picked up our pace and made quick time back to the car. "He's nowhere in sight," Nicole confirmed as I sped away from the parking lot. "Maybe it was just a coincidence. Maybe we're just spooked because of the guy that was killed?" she said hopefully.

I prayed she was right, but my gypsy senses were telling me otherwise.

HAM PITAS (OR ROLL UPS)

The absolute easiest recipe ever- and always a big hit. When I was a manager at an insurance company, my staff frequently requested that I make this on birthdays and during potlucks.

> 1 can flaked ham (I get the low sodium one)
> 1 heaping tablespoon mayonnaise (absolutely not miracle whip)
> Dash of garlic powder
> Dash or three of dill if you have any (not the seed, the green bits)
> 1 teaspoon of relish (optional- I hate relish but it's great in this recipe)

Drain the flaked ham, dumping the liquid down the sink, and mix everything together in a bowl. If you can find mini pitas (not always available), then slit them and fill with mixture. If you can't, I like to use different kinds of tortilla wraps. Spread on wrap, roll, then slice into 1 inch pieces. It tastes best if you let them chill for a few hours or overnight.

Judy Volhart

CHAPTER NINE

*O*kay, so I'm not really part gypsy. Or so my parents say. My childhood had been spent butting heads with them, I being born Canadian and they being mentally stuck in the "old country". I basically lived in lockdown, not being allowed to do, or say, very much. Surprisingly, I was not forced to wear a chastity belt. No doubt because they were simply not aware that such a contraption existed. But I digress.

Although I'm not clairvoyant, I would often have "feelings" about things and then something would happen. I seldom mention that I also saw ghost-like things during my childhood because that just makes me sound crazy and there are few believers out there.

There had not been any such sightings since becoming an adult, and for that I was thankful, especially considering I'd likely have at least one ghost rambling about in my house after the recent murders. In any case, I felt sure that there must be some gypsy blood somewhere in our ancestry.

My parents continue to vehemently deny this, although they begrudgingly let it slip that someone, years ago, had married a Jewish lady. My parents tend to be prejudiced and bigoted. Recently, I couldn't resist having a little fun at their expense.

I had gone home for a visit, bringing along a male friend of mine who had also just gone through a break-up and was feeling down. He was black, with longish hair in cornrows and wore an earring. All this combined was already horrific, in their view. While there, I told my parents he was also Jewish. And my new boyfriend. It wasn't true, but it's a moment I still relish—payback for all my unpleasant childhood memories. And for having to eat my pet rabbit. But I digress again.

So although I supposedly wasn't gypsy, I didn't believe it. I knew by now to trust my feelings and I was certain there was more to this guy downtown than mere coincidence. I just wish we'd gotten a better look at him, but I felt sure we'd see him again and the more I thought about it, the angrier I became.

I refused to feel unsafe, especially in my own home. Even so, I found myself frequently glancing out the windows, feeling prickly. Was I being watched? I put my thumbs in my ears and wiggled my fingers while sticking out my tongue. Watch me then.

Nicole caught my little display and raised her brows. "Problem?" she asked, looking around to see whom I might be targeting. I sighed, "Just going crazy, of course. I can't shake the feeling that we're being watched, and it's pissing me off! I hope it's not one of your ex-dates or something!" I joked feebly then felt uneasy, seeing her face twist in dismay.

She walked over to the blinds and closed them. "There; problem solved. If someone wants to watch us, they'll have to come inside and then they're on our turf". She, too, was growing angry. In fact, although I'm normally shy, I also have a feisty streak, but I pale in comparison to Nicole. Catching my jitters, she marched to the front door, yanked it open and glared out. I started to laugh and went over and hugged her. "Come on, Sparky, we've got work to do." As I dragged her back inside I thought I caught a blur of movement outside and quickly slammed and locked the door. We chatted distractedly while finishing the set-up for the evening, and I nervously peered out a couple of times, not seeing anything either time. I tried to tell myself that it was likely the cops were spying on me, and that did comfort me somewhat.

It was soon opening time and I found myself again staring at Matt's number that was written in the book. Now I was jittery and indecisive and I hated both feelings. I had to admit it, I was a chicken-shit. I didn't have the nerve to call Matt and knew I never would. And that, too, pissed me off. I'm normally a very strong willed person so I didn't like feeling weak or hesitant. I glared at the book, and then I glared at the blinds. Perhaps I'd never call Matt, but there was something I could do.

"Nicole, what do you say we head back downtown tomorrow?" She looked at me from the stage, where she had been dusting off the piano area. "Are you crazy?" she exclaimed. "And see that creep again?"

"Yes," I replied calmly. "That's exactly what I mean. In fact, I'm counting on it. If we keep seeing him, then we'll know he's after us and that it's not our imagination. And if he is, then it's got to have something to do with the murdered coat in my office or the man on my stairs."

I neglected to mention that if we did see him, I planned to try to turn the tables and follow him. I wasn't sure she'd like that idea. I wasn't sure I liked the idea either, but it was all I could come up with. My real estate agent still hadn't called me back so that lead was dead for now. I shuddered at the pun of my own making then had a mini panic attack. What if she was dead, too? Could that be why she wasn't calling?

The evening was an interesting one. We weren't packed, but it was busy enough and many people couldn't resist asking for details, admitting they'd read about what had happened in the local paper. Some even asked if they could see where it happened. I politely declined, not wanting the general public to be aware of my secret staircase. The paper hadn't mentioned those specifics, and I was thankful for that.

Speculation swirled and Nicole and I listened, smiled and served the customers. Like me, she'd jotted down what she'd overheard during the evening and at closing time we compared notes.

"Okay, so here's what we know", I said, as I peered out a corner of the blinds. Something I found myself doing during the course of the evening and had even caught Nicole doing it too. The street was deserted, parked cars long gone and very little traffic on Robin Road.

"The guy that was found on the steps was possibly a local business man, but that was purely speculation at this point. He hadn't shown up for a meeting with a husband and wife in town the other day and he'd had a reputation for being very punctual. If I understand correctly, he was also a handy man, so he'd have had access to people's houses. Not much dirt on him yet, but I did pick up more news on the first murder now that some time has passed." I paused for a deep breath before resuming my summary. I felt like I was in an episode of CSI.

"Victim number one: he may or may not have lived alone in the house in which he grew up. He may or may not have had a girlfriend. Sometimes someone would visit him. He went out every now and then but rarely spoke to anyone. He hadn't been seen in several weeks and was believed to be a hoarder (he certainly kept lots of junk in his yard, so speculation was that the inside was the same). Oh, and it seems he had quite a large plot of land that leads to the same trails that my land leads to." Here I faltered a bit, my bravado fizzling out. Although I did not vocalize it, that part worried me as it drew a direct link to me.

"We don't have much, do we?" Nicole sighed. "Oh, but

one more thing, someone may or may not be watching you, or us, and following you, or us." I took comfort in the "us" version.

"Thank you for that kind reminder." I shot her a glare and stopped myself from returning to the window. "So, in a way all this might be good. It means that very few people would have reason to kill the first guy, since he sounds like a hermit? The woman who was possibly a girlfriend, and the visitor that owned the car that was seen at his house. You'd think it would be easy for the cops to figure this one out." Even as I said this, I knew that I was likely over-simplifying since obviously they hadn't figured it out and now someone else was dead and I was likely the prime suspect. "Of course, there's my real estate agent, too, who knew this house was empty and was interested in buying it, and the former owners, as well as all the locals, some of whom might not be happy with me opening a business here, such as this Mr. Leonardo, and maybe even someone that viewed the house while it was for sale." Suddenly, the list seemed daunting. "And that doesn't even include the other dead man, and whoever took my money, and probably everyone who was here on New Year's Eve!"

What I didn't verbalize was that there was also a man here tonight that seemed intent on watching both Nicole and I, despite being in the company of a woman. Was my imagination running wild?

"Noon tomorrow?" I asked tightly, having completely creeped myself out.

"Well, I can't let you go alone, can I? But, how about one o'clock instead?" Nicole replied, on her way out the door. I sighed as she walked away and noticed her looking about nervously.

I locked up, checking everything twice. Three times. Peeking out the blinds. Checking the locks again. Making sure all the lights were off. Checked the locks again. Glared out the window, again. Sighed, again. Felt resentful. Then angry. Then scared, and angry again.

I stomped upstairs, the light in the stairwell now working as it had merely been a burnt bulb. The scent of pine stung my nostrils and tired eyes. I locked up and stood in the kitchen, looking around for ideas. Spotting my prey, I dragged the two kitchen stools over and placed them in front of the door. If someone managed to come up this way, I'd hear the chairs moving as the door opened, and there would be at least a bit of resistance.

I headed to my other door, the one at the top of the outdoor staircase. Although this was triple-locked, I still didn't feel safe. I was, after all, from Montreal, where we trusted no one and always kept our doors locked, even during the day. This small town wasn't like that, but under the present circumstances I could not imagine myself feeling safe enough to leave things unlocked.

I dragged all four chairs from my dining area over and placed them in front of that door, and that made me feel a bit better.

I dropped into bed, exhausted to the bone. The night had run later than usual and I was overdue for my thyroid pill. I had recently switched to taking it at nights, having read that the body might absorb it better. So far, my body did not agree as my every joint seemed to ache. Too tired to get anything for the pain, I closed my eyes and hoped for the best.

My overactive imagination going full throttle, I thought I kept hearing things. The crunch of snow outside (impossible, since I was on the upper level), thuds and thumps and squeaks. Finally, I drifted off to sleep, but in my dreams I found myself surrounded by chairs. I sat in the middle, with an empty bottle of vodka in one hand and a stinky Blue Stilton cheese in the other, both held as weapons. On top of the chairs were boxes piled high. Eyes watched me from between the chair legs. A goat bleated, its face the source of glaring eyeballs. Bleat. Bleat. Bleat.

Waking with a start, my hand shot out and turned off the "bleating" alarm. Always hating that alarm, I made a mental note to buy a new one, one that played music from the radio. I slowly creaked out of bed, feeling like death and wistfully remembering more energetic days.

I puttered about slowly, working the kinks out of my body while putting all the chairs and stools back in their proper places. I stood in the middle of the room for a while, uncertain what to do next. Was my subconscious trying to tell me something, or was I cracking under the strain?

Later, I picked up Nicole and we headed downtown. It was Saturday and the market was bustling with activity. I didn't notice anyone following us this time.

The temperature had warmed to an acceptable minus 5 Celsius. This was almost spring-like, a real treat. Although we walked about slowly, meandering through the market and along the streets surrounding it, we did not catch sight of the man from the day before.

By the end of our reconnaissance, we were giggling uncontrollably, laughing at ourselves and feeling a little more relaxed, and thinking perhaps, after all, we really had been wrong about being watched the day before.

Until we walked past a café and there, sitting at a table by the window, was Harriet with a man who was not her husband.

I had stopped dead in my tracks and quickly pulled up my hood, then picked up my pace. I'd only met Harriet once, but it was hard not to recognize her bright orange hair. Her husband, Harold, had a bald head with a few blond wisps that contrasted greatly with this man's great head of dark hair.

I caught up to Nicole. "Let's go across the street for minute. I just saw the former lady owner with someone and I want to get another peek." She gave me a curious look but followed me across the street. As we watched, they clinked glasses, laughed and held hands. "My, my, Harriet, you sly old gal," I muttered under my breath.

"But that's not the guy who was following us," Nicole

stated.

"No," I agreed. "But it's another puzzle, isn't it?" We watched for a moment then continued onward.

We returned to the bistro, hands empty, except for a new alarm clock (I had remembered, though I had forgotten the post-it note that I'd written it down on).

Another busy evening followed, the town lured outside by milder weather. While everyone was still buzzing about the new murder, we'd learned little, as most people didn't seem to know the deceased. One morsel did catch my attention though as I walked past a table. "...break-in about three or four weeks ago..." and then a lowered voice. I didn't catch the rest even though I hovered nearby. I made a note on my pad: "Break-in".

Another lock-up. Double check. Triple check. Peek out the blinds. Did I catch a glimpse of movement? Glare. The burning scent of pine in the stairway. Upstairs, placing the chairs and stools in front of the doors. Bone-numbing exhaustion. A brief thought: Was Hans right? Was running this place too much for me?

Having slept fitfully the past couple of days, I was asleep that night before my head hit the pillow. I was having one of my favorite dreams, the one in which I was eating my favorite foods and savoring every bite, when a large crash sent the cat and I both tumbling out of bed and to the floor.

We both froze, motionless and listening intently, not daring to breathe and then gasping for air. I slithered snake-like on my belly to peer around the edge of the bed, where I could look out my open doorway into the hallway. Shadows loomed but nothing moved. After an eternity, I crept, still on my belly, to the doorway. I peeked out then crept further. Hummer darted past, almost giving me a stroke.

Feeling vulnerable on the floor, I slowly raised myself into a crouching position, my already sore knees screeching in protest. I moved toward the living room.

Then I saw the rock on the floor. It didn't seem like anyone was there, but that some spineless toad had thrown a rock my way. Probably some teenagers causing havoc, which I had recently learned wasn't uncommon in the area.

I went back to the bedroom, got my bat and cell phone and switched on the flashlight app. Deja-vu with the flashlight app. Shudder.

Just in case someone was watching, I didn't want them to see me turning on lights. Back to the rock. I aimed the light from my phone and froze: *Peek-a-boo. ICU.*

I killed the flashlight app and hit the floor.

CHAPTER TEN

Only one cop car came this time, having taken a good hour to arrive. The rock had not killed me, or anyone else, therefore there was no urgency. No officers were present from the previous visit, meaning I had to rehash the events of both murders, in order to attach greater significance to The Rock.

I earned a nod for my efforts—he had thankfully heard of the murders. He looked at me curiously, or perhaps it was with pity, I wasn't sure. Maybe it was suspicion. I was promised some infrequent drive-by surveillance. I raised a brow, knowing I was already under surveillance and wondering where they had been tonight. For now, they would canvass the area but were not optimistic they would find anything. He let it slip that there was talk that the recent murder may have been in connection to some burglaries in the area and then politely recommended I get a security system. He did not scowl or frown or raise eyebrows.

I was more cautious that day, not venturing out and just spending the day taking down holiday decorations, planning menus and shopping lists for the coming weeks, scribbling thoughts and notes to myself that I would no doubt misplace. The window repair put a dent not only in my budget but in my mood and no doubt my heating bill as it took forever to get the old house warmed again. I moped about for a while, allowing myself a couple of hours to wallow in self- pity.

By the time Nicole arrived to help me open, I was practically bursting with pent-up energy and agitation. I filled her in on the latest, not having called her earlier since, after all, it was just a rock. Plus she had a life—she had hinted about a lunch date—and I didn't want to intrude.

A few in the evening crowd had heard about the rock and speculation bubbled. How does the news travel so fast, I wondered?! Obviously, I still did not realize how small towns functioned.

A brunette with hooker make-up, sparkling eyes and milky white chest spilling out of her top grabbed my wrist as I passed: "Sweetie, you poor thing, you must be worried! Do you think this person is after you? Two murders, a rock and a burglary? You really should get some protection!"

Seeing my confused expression, she continued. "I have a cousin who works as a bodyguard in his spare time. I can give him a call if you like. He's actually the one that recommended I come here; he just loves the place. I'm sure if you paid him with food, he'd be happy!" She cackled, and then to my horror, she zipped out her cell and punched in a number then flapped me away after giving a thumbs-up sign.

Later, on her way out, she assured me that her cousin would swing by when he had a chance to talk to me about my security needs. I couldn't help but grin at my own thoughts as she yammered a mile a minute. And then she was gone.

"Mind if I zip out now?" Nicole asked hopefully. "If you need me, I'll stay, but I was up early this morning and

I feel like death." I had noticed dark circles under her eyes earlier and wondered if something else was going on. Since I could handle the clean-up, I sent her on her way.

Intent on my new OCD routine of checking all locks two or ten times, I failed to notice movement until the last moment, when I suddenly looked up to see a face pressed against the glass, directly in front of mine. I screeched. I even peed a little.

The face backed away from the door, smiling. Okay, laughing. A hand rose in a friendly hello as I recognized him.

Not sure what was going on, I approached the door. I was about to unlock it when I hesitated. Okay, so I knew him. Well, kind of. But what if he was the killer?

He'd already been here a couple of times. Maybe he had another motive. What was he doing here? Was he angry that I hadn't called? Would he kill me? Bludgeon me with a rock? I was so jumpy that everyone was now a suspect—even Nicole, with her strange behavior of late. Okay, maybe not Nicole, I scolded myself. I'd known her since I was twelve. She wouldn't have waited eighteen years to kill me. She was far too impatient for that.

"May I help you?" I said loudly, hoping he could hear me through the closed door.

"I'm here to help you," I lip-read. Actually, I lie. I'm a horrible lip-reader and I thought he said "I'm here for you." I stood still, unsure of what to do. Then I heard him bellow something about a cousin. It clicked: the hooker's cousin.

I unlocked and opened the door, suddenly shy, and stood aside to let Keith Urban inside. I caught a subtle scent of cologne, took in the longish, sandy hair, the lean body, jeans, a nice shirt under his unbuttoned coat. And then I started babbling.

"I'm so sorry, it's really not urgent, it was just a stupid rock and I don't even know your cousin, didn't even get a chance to say much, and then she was on the phone and then she was gone and here you are..." my voice trailed off.

Matt leaned back against my bar counter, an amused little smile tugging at the corners of his lips. He leaned forward and held out his hand. "We haven't officially met, have we? I'm Matt". Not Keith. Of course, I knew that.

I shook his hand, mumbling my name in return.

"It's nice to meet you Amalia. That's a beautiful name. Helen, my cousin, told me about what happened. I'm sorry you're having all these problems. The first murder was particularly disturbing. It just so happens that I've taken a couple of weeks' vacation from work and have some spare time, if you'd like me to stick around and make sure nothing happens."

I peeked out at him from beneath my bangs. Oh yeah baby! Instead, I stammered, "But won't your girlfriends worry?" Where had that come from? Whose mouth was this, anyway? Get me a muzzle.

Matt threw back his head and laughed a full belly laugh. When he was done, he grinned. "Is that why you never called me?"

Oh no! I was hoping not to have this conversation. "Um, well, actually, the money with your number was stolen that night by whoever broke in." I left it at that. There was no need for him to know about the reservation book.

"So, you're saying maybe you would have called me then?" he said with another grin. That irritating, throbbing bolt of lightning chose that moment to sluice through my left temple. As my face slightly contorted, his grin fell. I had to explain, fast, before he misinterpreted my look.

"Sorry, headache. Ummmmm.....I'm not sure if I would have called. You were here with two different girls. Not that I would have really noticed, except both had red claws—I mean, nails—that seemed permanently attached to your wrists, and...." I wasn't quite sure what else to say. "Well, I don't date....much... I mean....sure I do, all the time....but if...when... I do....and I do a lot...one person at a time. And I expect the same". There. I managed to spit it out as gracefully as I could. My face flaming, I bowed my head so my long hair could shield me.

To my horror, he began laughing again. My head snapped up, my temper flickering to life. "Listen, "I sputtered, "I don't go for players. If that's what you are, that's fine, I don't judge, but that's just not the type of person I go for, and I have more self-respect than to be Ms. Wednesday Night".

"Fair enough," he replied, still smiling. "How about a date for Tuesday night then—I think you're closed that night, right?" He obviously wasn't getting it.

"Keith...Matt, that's not what I meant. I'm uh....not into the harem thing."

Again, he laughed but finally took mercy on me. He leaned forward and reached out a finger, hooking it around my curtain of hair that I was furiously trying to hide behind, and tucking it behind my ear. He was close. I could smell his cologne again and could feel waves of heat encroaching on me, almost singeing my skin. My stomach clinched and tingled as my eyes widened. We looked at each other for what seemed like an eternity. Suddenly, he stepped back, clearing his throat. Without looking at me, he spoke: "So you date a lot? I don't. The dates were blind dates." Now he was stammering. "My friend figured I needed to do something other than work, hike and cycle, and that I should get back into the dating world. Seriously, did those girls look like they even like the outdoors? And you're right about the claws. I swear I found marks on my wrist. And for the record, I hadn't dated in about a year and have no plans to see either of them again. Nor have any more blind dates."

He was the one with his face down now, talking to the floor. I envisioned my hand reaching out to brush his hair off his forehead. Instead, I stood frozen.

"Okay," I said quietly.

"Okay?" he asked, confused.

"Tuesday night," I replied. "That's in two days. Yes, I'm off. But I'm not sure I need a bodyguard. I have a very sophisticated security system upstairs, so even if someone gets in down here, it's unlikely I'd be in danger upstairs." A tiny lie. I compensated by coming clean about the dating. "And I actually don't date very much either; at least not lately."

"Fair enough", he replied. And then, "Do you mind if I look around? You know, in case I happen to be passing by, if I see anyone lurking about, I'll know the lay of the land, so I know that you're safe and snug? And by the way, did you know there's someone out there now? Some guy in a car..."

Double damn! The ex, and now he'd find out that I was lying about a security system. But there was no way out of it.

"It's probably my ex from ages ago. He thinks I'm suddenly flush with money. He thinks he can intimidate me. Come on, I'll show you around." I gave him the tour and he inspected windows and doors closely. We arrived at my secret staircase and I took out my keys to unlock the two locks.

"My secret passage", I explained, "and where the person was found dead on my stairs. The other was back here, in my office," I gestured. A shadow crossed his face but was quickly gone. He asked if it was locked the night of the murder and I admitted that in my exhaustion, I must have forgotten.

We arrived at the top, which I had left unlocked during the day (since the bottom had been properly secured). Once inside, we stood in the kitchen while Hummer blinked at us in disgust.

I see we have company, Hummer blinked at me accusingly. I made the introductions and described Hummer as my guard cat, recapping his actions the night of the murder. Matt did not look convinced and continued his investigation of my premises.

"So where is the security system that you mentioned earlier?" I pointed at Hummer, and then I pointed at the chairs. Wordlessly, I demonstrated by moving the chairs and stools into place, then turned to face him, smiling wide, arms spread. "Ta-da!"

He nodded politely. "I see. So, Tuesday... Five o'clock, right? I'll pick you up and we can go out for dinner? And if you need me before then, I'll be around. I know your security is top of the line," he grinned, "but I'll just make sure no one's hanging around."

My stomach did that little flip-flop thing again. I had a date! And I'd likely see him before then! I agreed to five o'clock but did not comment about him possibly scoping my place out. Discussing that and payment and dating all at the same time would be awkward. As it was, it was awkward enough. While I hated to part from him, I also couldn't wait to get him out of there. I'd had all the excitement I could take.

I showed him out on the inner stairs so that we could both do one last check of the locks. At the door, he turned at the last second, looking at me for a moment. Without comment, he picked up one of my hands and laid it palm-down in his own, holding my hands up for inspection. He nodded and grinned. "Perfect", he said. "No claws. Just the way I like it". And with that, he stepped out and waited for me to lock the door and give him the thumbs-up sign.

I went back upstairs, locking all locks and bolts along the way and came to halt in the kitchen. Hummer was on the counter, no doubt a strategic ploy to be closer to eye level with me. *What do you think you're doing?* I imagined him saying.

I grinned at him. "Deal with it, Hum. I have a date!" He scowled as I skipped to the shower.

I had a date! And I wouldn't be Ms. Wednesday Night! I did a naked little cha-cha-cha, singing "La Cucaracha" just because it had a cha-cha-cha tune. Hip thrust; oh yeah! Butt thrust; oh yeah! A little Miley-style twerk: I had

YouTube'd it once and I clearly needed more practice.

Suddenly I stopped. I felt that creepy-crawly feeling. I grabbed a towel and went to the window to have a final peek outside and saw a car parked in the lot. I let go of the blind.

I peeked again and caught his profile as the headlights of a passing car lit him. Matt was leaning in through the ex's window and having a chat. While I watched, the headlights came on and the car screeched away. Matt got into his car and waited. I had that creepy-crawly feeling again. But wait! This was a different creep, a different crawl. I scooted back to the bathroom for a shower and to shave my legs. This called for a fresh blade.

This might be a good time for a snack. It's good to get up and stretch every now and then. How about a plate of nachos?

NACHOS

Tortilla chips
Salsa
Onions, green & red pepper
Meat (diced and cooked chicken, steak or hot dog)
Olives, if you must (hate 'em)
Cheese of choice
Sour cream

Get out one dinner-sized plate. Spread a layer of tortilla chips so that none of them overlap each other. On each one, placed a small teaspoon of your favorite salsa. Then, top with chopped green onions, or regular onions if you prefer, some chopped red and green pepper. If you have leftover steak, chicken or even hot dogs, chop them up and spread them around. Next, layer on a good amount of grated cheese. I like cheddar or the Habanero Heat pre-shredded cheese.

Nuke in the microwave for about 2 minutes. You don't want to overdo it. If the cheese isn't melty, do another 30 seconds. Enjoy with sour cream. Cha cha cha.

Want more? Make another plate- don't make a double
layer on one plate, it's not as good.

CHAPTER ELEVEN

*T*he next afternoon I tried to call Janet. No answer again. My apprehension and imagination grew to the point where I almost expected to find her body stashed somewhere in my house.

Although it was Monday, we had our first special event so we were open. With my severance pay soon coming to an end, the panic was starting to set in so I figured a special event would draw in a bit of extra cash.

Men's Monday was in full swing, and the local hockey team was in town. Their every move was watched avidly on the big screen TV I had splurged on when the Boxing Day sales proved too good to resist. Stephen had come for a quick visit and helped me to install it right in the middle of the giant chalkboard wall by the bar.

Since the idea had come to us only a few days ago, I had not placed an ad in the local paper, but had merely placed a sign out front near the road. It worked.

We'd moved some of the furniture around to make it more "manly", arranging all the couches and club chairs together in a manner where everyone could see the screen. The high tables and stools were placed farthest from the

TV.

Matt came by with his friend Ricky, and while he wasn't bad looking, he had slightly bulgy eyes and brillo-pad curly dark hair. His high cheekbones and pleasant smile made up for the eyes and hair. He raised not one but two eyebrows at my evening's choice of T-shirt, which had been Nicole's daring idea: *Ask me about our Ménage a Trois*. I smiled sweetly then explained that it was a wine, of course, and proceeded to tell them a little about its merits. "A fruity, silky blend of Zinfandel, Merlot and Cab," I defined.

I had something else in mind for them though. "I'll be back in just a moment with something for you," I said with a wink, then went off to prepare one of my staple menu items. Crumbly Goat cheese drizzled with a sundried tomato concoction, creamy double brie, multigrain baguette hunks, thick slabs of Cervelat and German salamis and a garlic and herb pâté, adorned with some artfully scattered green and purple grapes, strawberries and a handful of almonds.

Remembering that Ricky (Tonsils) drank white and Matt drank red, I poured an extra generous glass of white Fish Eye and a tall order of red Sexy. "Enjoy, it's on the house," I said quietly, then leaned over to whisper to Matt, "Thanks for keeping watch last night and getting rid of *him*." And with that, I sashayed away with a little extra Canadian "ay" in my walk. His eyes practically bore a hole in my backside.

Just as I was mentally complimenting myself on my newfound flirting abilities, my hip bumped one of the club chairs. My step faltered but I regained my balance just in time. I dared not take a peek to see if Matt was still watching. Busying myself by repositioning the chair and cleaning a side table, my gaze shifted to the arrival of more customers.

I watched in barely concealed horror as the somewhat sexy, Mr. Scowly officer number two, Sean, sauntered in with a couple of other men. He was not in uniform, so I took this to mean that this was not an official call, and my hopes for news on the murder were quickly dashed. Perhaps I was still under surveillance. I scowled then raised a brow. Beat that!

He surprised me with a jovial smile, "Ma'am." That was it. Mr. Conversation himself! They found some newly vacated club chairs and settled in. I rushed to the back, where Nicole was preparing platters of nachos.

"Officer Sean is here with some friends", I casually mentioned.

Her face lit up. "Oh, how nice," she attempted to say casually. "We're sure to be safe tonight." With that, she loaded the platters and breezed by me, her cheeks so red I debated getting the fire extinguisher ready.

The rest of the evening was uneventful but busy. As the hockey game came to an end, I went around settling bills and alternated between stealing peeks at Matt, deep in conversation with Ricky, and Officer Sean, whose eyes were transfixed on Nicole.

Other than polite exchanges, Matt and I did not speak, not wanting to tip anyone off that we knew each other. Most people in town knew him, and word would spread quickly if they suspected that he was helping me. Assuming the murderer would be fairly local, it would be best to keep things under wraps.

Matt and Ricky were getting ready to leave when Matt said, "You go on ahead, buddy, I've got to use the men's room. Talk to you later this week." Ricky departed and a few minutes later Matt waited casually by the bar while I said goodbye to other customers.

"I'll be back in a couple of hours to keep an eye on things", he said.

Meanwhile, Nicole sat down with Officer Sean, his friends having left a few minutes earlier. Although they weren't touching, they had pulled the chairs a bit closer, and as I watched, Nicole threw her head back and I could hear her laugh. She was petite, but one thing that was not demure about her was her laugh. She had a big voice and an even bigger laugh, one that often turned heads. I smiled to myself. Oh yeah, I knew that laugh.

Later, as we tidied, I noticed she made sure to pretty much be wherever I wasn't. Finally, I stomped on over to her. Toes tapping, fingers wiggling, I said, "Give it to me. Every detail. And why don't I already know all this?"

A flush stained her cheeks...again. "So, we've had a couple of dates, mostly breakfast ones, but you know me and how things seldom make it to date three or four, so I didn't want to say anything until I was sure, and you didn't seem to like him so there really wasn't any point, and I've still been meeting some other guys too..."

I grabbed her. "Stop! Breathe! You sound like a runaway train. And I'm happy for you. He couldn't take his eyes off you."

"Ommagod, he's so hot!" she blurted. Yep, I knew it. I was right about that laugh. We poured ourselves a glass of OMG red and sat in the cozy chairs where she and Sean had sat.

Savoring the blend of Merlot, Syrah and Cabernet while chatting, she caught me up on what had been going on during the past few days. I did the same. At the end, we sat there grinning at each other like a couple of twelve-year-olds. No further talking was necessary and we sat back and just enjoyed our wine. The beginning of a new relationship is always exciting. To be starting one at the same time as your best friend; that's awesome!

Minutes after I locked up behind her, I heard knocking at the front door. I shimmied over quietly and peered around an edge of the blind, expecting to see Matt. My heart nearly stopped and I looked around for a weapon, just in case. I grabbed a candle off a table. It would have to do.

I opened the door cautiously and pasted a smile on my face. "Janet, my goodness, you're here late. I was starting to worry about you. I've been trying to call you for weeks.

Come in." I gripped the candle for dear life but took a bit of comfort in knowing Matt would be by at some point and would surely notice a car out front.

"I'm so sorry I couldn't get back to you sooner. I got your messages and I was in the area so I thought I'd take a chance and stop in. Too bad I didn't catch you while you were still open." My senses tingled. No one, and I mean no one, happens to ever be "in this area" since there's really nothing in the area to be at, unless you live here, so what she was saying couldn't be true.

"Oh, well, thank you for coming by. Why don't you have a seat and I'll get you some wine." I returned shortly with a glass of The Velvet Devil for her. I wasn't sure what to make of her yet, after all.

She gratefully took a long swallow and let out a purr of delight. "So, what did you need to see me about?" She got right to the point.

"Would you know if the former owners were friends with the owner of the pizza place, Mr. Leonardo? Harriet had mentioned that he'd been here once and had walked in on her while she was in the bath."

She started to laugh. "Oh, they told me that story too. They used to be friends, actually. Harriet and Harold opened this place first, and Leonardo really liked the area. Once he opened his business, this place took a hard hit. It never really did well to begin with, you see. After that, I think the friendship ended pretty fast."

"He seems to hate me and I haven't even met him yet. Would you have any idea why?" I prodded further.

"I'd imagine he's worried now that you'll put him out of business. That would be my guess."

"Did you know the first man that was murdered?"

"The first man? What do you mean, first?" she asked.

"Well, there was another one, on New Year's Eve. I guess you haven't heard." She blanched then shook her head quickly, pausing only to take a long swallow of wine.

"I was also wondering if you could tell me more about

why you were thinking about buying this place." I tried to slip that one in casually.

She had been in the middle of another long swig and started coughing as her head snapped up in surprise. "My God, you think I'm somehow linked to the murders, don't you?" She lurched to her feet, startling me. "I've never been so insulted in my life," she sputtered and stormed out despite my protest.

I quickly bolted the door. That hadn't gone as planned but her reaction was sure puzzling. Why would she automatically assume that I was hinting that she might be involved, even though I secretly may have been thinking it?

Early the next morning, I drove slowly past the hoarder's house a few times, the man rumoured to have been found in my home when I moved in. I wasn't quite sure what I was expecting to see, but at the very least I hoped to catch a glimpse of someone loitering about, other than me of course. I got lucky on the second drive-by when I saw a red SUV in the driveway. I drove by a few more times, hoping to catch a glimpse of whoever owned it, but with no luck. By my seventh pass, the car was gone.

I returned home, and since it was only 11:00 a.m., I crawled back into bed and languished with my second cup of coffee, relaxing while watching the Food Network from the comfort of my warm bed. This was my all-time favorite part of each day, especially on days when the bistro wasn't open. I have never been a morning person, and this routine suited me perfectly. I had six hours left to get ready for my date with Matt, which meant I had loads of time to dawdle.

The doorbell shrilled, causing me to spill coffee on myself but missing the blanket. I was not expecting company, nor was I in the mood for any. Anyone who knew me knew that I wasn't fond of having my mornings interrupted. And I had one hour left of morning-time. My eyes widened in horror. No! That could only mean one thing.

I leapt out of bed, swearing. Crap! Crap! Crap! No! I went to my door, the one that leads to the outside stairway, and there they were, in all their glory, my parents.

Bazd meg!

There's a word you might as well learn now. Familiarize yourself with it. Roll it around on your tongue. It's pronounced similar to "Buzzed Meg". Emphasis on the 'Buzzed'. It is the only word that every friend and boyfriend I've ever had bothered to learn. It is the equivalent to the almighty English F-bomb.

Don't get me wrong; it's not that I don't like my parents. I like them plenty when they are at least a hundred and sixty miles away. And quite frankly, it was still too early in the day to speak in Hungarian.

Unlike other Hungarians I knew growing up in Canada, my parents never spoke to us kids in English. I began learning English and French only at the age of five, and to this day, spoke in Hungarian (now peppered with English) only with my parents. Their English was very poor, especially my mother's.

I plastered a giant smile on face and unlocked the door. *"Szia Amalia!"* Hello. Big kisses. I imagined that I felt my mother's two whiskers graze my cheek and shuddered. I'd have to find a way to talk to her about that. "We thought we'd surprise you with a visit. Stephen said you're open on weekends only, so we thought we'd have a couple of days together," said my dad. A couple of days? Oh, God! No! And not today! My date with Matt!

"A couple of days? Great! This will be my first week where I start opening on Thursdays. Well, come on in, I'll show you around then we'll have some food and coffee." I took their bags and brought them to the spare room, giving a quick tour along the way. To my surprise, they complimented me on my little home. We went down via the secret passage and again, I was shocked to receive compliments on my bistro.

Here's the thing: Growing up, I was never encouraged to do anything I showed an interest in. A psychologist? No, don't be stupid, no one goes to see a psychologist; don't waste your time. Be an accountant; you'll make good money. I had barely passed math, so how could I be an accountant? Be a secretary; everyone needs a secretary. But I don't want to be a secretary. Then be an accountant. I wanted to join the drama club. That's stupid; a waste of time. Learn accounting. I joined the drama club anyway.

Having everything I needed downstairs, I seated them in some comfy chairs and brought them some coffee to perk them up. They lived in a suburb south of Montreal so they had been driving for two and a half hours.

Letting them relax, I ducked back into the kitchen to prepare some food and to squelch my impending panic attack. I would have to call Matt, tell him I'd meet him downtown, not to pick me up. It was too soon for him to meet the Aliens.

Ah, The Aliens! That is what my brother and I affectionately called my parents, behind their backs, of course, and for a plethora of reasons. Our parents refused to become Canadian in any way, shape or form and were so drastically different from everyone else that they didn't even own jeans, or allow us kids to wear them.

Our childhood was unlike that of other children, particularly mine, being female and thus requiring that my "virtue" be protected. I lived inside a bubble.

Satisfied with my plan of action, I ran to the reservation book and looked up Matt's number while grabbing the cordless phone that was underneath the bar. "I'll be out in a just a minute; I just need to make a quick business call." From the kitchen, I hastily dialed his number, hoping to just leave a message.

But he answered on the first ring, surprise in his voice. Call display. "Well, hello. I thought you lost my number." Damn. I forgot.

"Yes, that's true, but then I thought of the reservation

book, remembering you were here on New Year's Eve and that maybe we might have your number in there. And bingo, there it was! Lucky me!"

"Is everything okay? You're not cancelling, are you?"

"No, yes...I mean, everything's okay, and no I'm not cancelling. I just need to change things slightly. I'll meet you there, okay?"

Sensing tension in my voice, he said, "May I ask why?"

I sighed. If I'm going to date this guy, I might as well be honest. "The Aliens are here," I said.

"Did you say *Aliens*?"

"Sorry, I mean my parents. They just showed up. I'll spare you the experience and just meet you downtown".

To my dismay, he insisted on picking me up and nothing I could say would dissuade him. Sighing in resignation, I hung up then plastered my smile firmly in place and brought the food out to my parents.

We exchanged small talk in between mouthfuls. I knew they would have no issue with the food—this was the fair from my childhood: Hungarian salami, rye bread and Oka cheese. They asked about Hans. I told him he was crazy then asked about their various ailments. They asked about my finances, and I distracted them with more questions about their ailments. That tactic almost always worked. Then the inevitable: Had I met anyone yet? Here was my opening.

"Well. I do have a date tonight. Sorry, I'll have to leave you on your own for a couple of hours. This is my first date with him, so I didn't want to cancel. He'll be picking me up at five o'clock. Here."

A dozen questions, most of them answered with I dunno. And then, "Is he Hungarian?"

"No."

"Why not?"

"Because he's English".

"You need a good Hungarian boy."

"I don't want a Hungarian".

"Why not?"

"Because this is Canada".

My dad shook his head and repeated my name sadly a couple of times. He would get over it; he'd had a lifetime of me not living up to his expectations. Remember, I am not an accountant.

I changed the topic. "Anything in particular you want to do while you're here?"

Their reply was one I would never have expected to hear.

Bazd meg!!!!

CHAPTER TWELVE

*I*t was impossible. There must be something wrong with my hearing. Perhaps a sudden virus in my ears. My head throbbed, sending blood to my ears so all I could hear was thump, thump, thump. They looked at me expectantly, big happy smiles on their faces. How could my gypsy senses not have warned me?

I asked them to repeat.

"We want to look at some houses", my dad said. "Mama and I are thinking of moving here".

"Why? I mean, it's so expensive here in Ottawa, so much more than in Quebec."

No, no, no! This was a nightmare.

They explained that they were tired of the threat of separatism (some of Quebec's French population had been lobbying for decades for the province to split from the rest of Canada and neither of my parents spoke French).

"Won't you miss your friends?" I knew I was grasping at straws.

"We don't see much of them anymore. Some are dead, and some have moved back to the Old Country."

"Wow. This is just so....unexpected," I replied, at a loss

for words. "I can call the real estate agent that sold me this house and have her show you around Ottawa." Yes, that would give me a chance to make amends and maybe get more information out of her. And I would make sure she showed them houses on the opposite side of Ottawa, far, far away.

I called Janet, leaving a long message and apologizing profusely for the misunderstanding. I explained that because of the second murder I was just nervous but that I certainly did not suspect her and valued her friendship. What I really valued was any information she could think of that might help, and that had been my intent with the questions I'd asked. I then mentioned that my parents wanted to see some properties, gave her the specifics and underlined the importance of ensuring they were as far away as possible from the town of Robin.

Moments after I hung up she returned my call and apologized in return for being so defensive, explaining that she'd been under a lot of personal strain lately. She assured me that she'd do her best to help my parents find a house and said she'd stop by the following morning to get them.

Heaving a sigh of relief, I led them back upstairs and made sure they were comfortable, which meant turning the heat up to 26 degrees Celsius. Feeling my throat already closing up from the heat, I changed into a tank top and shorts then made sure the spare bed had fresh sheets. Then, it was time to prepare for The Date.

At 4:59, Matt knocked on the door. I resisted the urge to plead with my parents to be normal and simply wished for the best.

In English: "Matt, this is my mom, Julia, and my dad Zoltan. Mom, Dad, this is Matt."

"Hallo, Mutt," said my mother.

Cringe.

My father: "Hallo, ha varrrr you?" Translated, how are you?

"Nice to meet you. Will you be staying here for a few

days?"

"Ya, ya, ve looking for house to moving here." my father replied.

"Okay, good night, folks", I interrupted. "We have a reservation and we'll be late. Dad, here's the remote. My phone is in the kitchen if you need to call me, and don't wait up for me!"

Yeah, right...

"Vat time you coming to home?" Mom asked.

"Not sure, Mom, but don't worry. I'm a big girl. Good night."

I practically pushed Mutt out the door and hurried after him. "Hurry," I urged. He chuckled but obeyed and bolted down the stairs. At the bottom, he grabbed my hand and we ran to his car. Once inside, we burst out laughing.

"And there you have it, Mutt. The Aliens. You survived."

"Well, you hardly gave us a chance to get to know each other. They seem like nice people. So is that a good thing, them wanting to move here?"

"Drive, now, before they come after us! And no, it's not a good thing."

I leaned back in his car and felt the heated seats warming my backside. That was nice—unless the warmth was because I had wet myself without realizing it. "Heated seats?" I asked cautiously, relaxing only once he confirmed that they were.

I resumed our conversation. "No, not a good thing. If they're local, it means having to call them every day instead of once a week. If I miss a day, I'll be hearing from them the next, with some sort of snide comment, plus I'll have to see them at least once a week. If they live closer than thirty minutes away, I'll have to see them more often. Or worse yet, they'll come to see me, and then it's harder to cut the visit short. And then there will be the constant interest in my life, comments, judgments, prodding me to learn accounting..." I trailed off, too depressed to continue.

He gave me a sympathetic look, but the twitching at the corner of his lips gave him away. I glared at him and snapped, "Let's change the subject".

He let me stew a while, his lips still twitching. We drove around downtown, trying to find parking. Giving up, he parked in the same indoor lot where I usually park, then we went the rest of the way on foot.

Soon, we were seated and waiting for our appetizers, happily sipping a glass of wine. Something about a Chateau and the Pope. Not particularly funny. What kind of place was this?

"Okay. Your turn under the spotlight, since you're so amused by my life", I said to Matt.

"Amused? I didn't say a word."

"You were snickering to yourself at my expense the whole ride here. Don't even try to deny it!" I tried to look testy, but in all honesty the wine was quickly loosening my tongue. "So, tell me about yourself. What do you do?"

"I work for a security company."

"Do you mean the body guarding thing? I thought your cousin said you used to do that, past tense."

"Yes, past tense, mostly, but I still do it sometimes. Now I dabble in other things."

Other things? Was he embarrassed by his job? I switched to a less invasive topic. "Are you from around here?"

To my surprise he was born and raised in Ottawa, which is rare. Most of the people I know are from somewhere else but end up here. He'd grown up here but had moved to British Columbia for a few years, and then moved back to Ottawa. "Why did you come back?" At this point, the wine no longer cared if I asked more personal questions.

"Bad break-up. Missed my folks, friends, cousins. There was nothing there for me that I couldn't do here. My parents are pretty cool; they travel a lot. I have two sisters. I'm the baby. And a whole herd of cousins—my mom comes from a family of nine kids. They're spread out all over the place." His voice drifted off and his brows came down in a flicker of a scowl as he looked just past me. I had noticed his eyes had been shifting about and figured maybe he was nervous, or worse, disinterested.

I nonchalantly took a glance behind me and saw a raven-haired beauty at a table nearby. I suppose if I were a male, my eyes would have shifted her way too. I pushed back the sudden feeling of disappointment and pasted a smile on my face.

He began speaking again: "I visited Joey about a month ago. I still can't believe he's dead." I looked at him blankly. Were we having the same conversation? Had I blacked out at some point? Joey?

"The man on your...coat hooks," he stammered and looked at me sadly. "We were best friends in elementary school, at the age when you don't realize other kids are different. As we got older, he kept to himself a lot and I think I'm pretty much the only friend that ever went over there. I tried to keep in touch over the years, tried to talk him into getting help. But he was happy just the way he was."

The sudden realization jolted me out of my partly drunk stupor as I remembered the red SUV that had been parked in front of the hoarder's house. It had been Matt's!

"So when my cousin asked me to help you, the answer was easy; I didn't think twice."

Sensing Matt's sadness, I didn't intrude with further questions about Joey, although I wanted to ask why he didn't tell me this sooner.

We continued to chat about more neutral topics. School, previous jobs, pets. He seemed quite distracted. Finally I lost patience. "Okay, what's up? If you're not having a good time, we can go. Or perhaps you'd prefer to join the lady at her table?"

His gaze snapped over to me in surprise. "I didn't realize...I'm sorry. No, I don't want to go. And why would

I want to join someone else?" He studied me for a moment, my mouth a thin gash as I glared at him, offended by his interest in anything other than me. I thought I'd done a pretty good job of dolling myself up for him. I had worked for a good half hour at straightening my long hair that normally had some natural waves in it and putting on a little extra makeup, working quite a while at the smoky eye, being out of practice. The least he could do was gaze lovingly at me, or if not that, then at least look at me like he was somewhat interested. He cast another glance at the door then leaned toward me and took my hand in his. Smiling, he said as quietly as possible, "I don't want to scare you, but I think we were followed here. I didn't get a very good look from here, but I got the feeling a man was watching us the whole time. He just left about three minutes ago. I could be wrong though, and maybe he wasn't alone, so I didn't want to say anything, but trust me, I do not want to leave."

The heat from his hand shot up my arm. Into my shoulder. Down to my stomach and traveled south of my belly button ring. Flushed from my mid-section to my eyebrows, I almost got lost in his brilliant green eyes. I watched his lips moving and pictured them brushing my skin. Suddenly his words registered and I remembered the reason we'd met in the first place. Somehow I'd managed to forget that an innocent person had been murdered, and that I was being followed.

I snatched my hand away and gripped the table. "Matt! We have to go. My parents! I didn't tell them. What if something happens?" He reached back across the table and reclaimed my hand.

"Nothing will happen. I have it covered. Remember, I used to do this for a living. Ricky works with me, and I asked him to hang around your house for a couple of hours tonight while we were out, just in case. With the free booze and food you gave us the other night, he was happy to repay the favor." The heat shot out its pulsing rays as his thumb stroked my hand.

We split a dessert, had some coffee, and shared some laughs, the atmosphere more relaxed now. He recounted the details of the two blind dates he'd been on in my bistro. I wondered why he chose that location.

"Well, the first night, I was curious about your place, since you had just opened. For the second date..." he faltered then cleared his voice, "okay, for the second date, I figured if it bombed, which it did, I'd at least have you to look at."

Hello!

"And hence the phone number?"

"Yeah. After five minutes there, with her claws stuck in my skin, I knew it was doomed. And, well, you looked pretty damned good. You were wearing a t-shirt that said 'Wild Thing'. Halfway through the date, I went to the men's room and wrote my number on a bill and just waited for my chance to slip it to you." He grinned sheepishly.

Blushing, I reminded him that the t-shirts we wear are all names of wines, or have something to do with the Whine and Cheese, and how we try to be witty. I shared how I thought he was a two-timer, and how horrified I was when he gave me his number and thought he wanted me as Ms. Wednesday night, and wondered if he had someone tucked away for each night of the week. Laughing, he admitted that those had been his first two dates in a very long time, and I was his third.

Third time lucky, I hoped, and felt guilty for thinking he'd been checking out the raven-haired lady behind us.

"By the way," he leaned in to whisper in my ear after paying the bill, "the lady with the black hair is a dude." He grinned then stood, extending his hand to me. As we passed the table I snuck a peak. He was right!

We strolled back to the car, hand in hand. People bustled around us and the snow had started falling again. He put on a winter hat, while I pulled my hood over my head, knowing what my hair would look like if it got wet.

That natural wave would spring back to life and turn unevenly kinky. Not a pretty sight, and I'll be the first to admit that I can be vain at times.

With our senses alert to the potential of being followed, we both scanned the area. We got to the car and back home safely, satisfied that we weren't tailed, and Matt suggested that perhaps he'd just been paranoid. Ricky pulled away from the side of the road a few feet past my house, where he'd set up watch. He gave us a thumbs-up before driving away.

As we got out of the car, I looked at the windows upstairs and was not surprised to see my mom standing there looking out at me. She shook a finger. I got the message loud and clear, as if she'd shouted it. "No hanky-panky; I'm watching." I groaned. Flashbacks to my youth.

Matt walked me to the bottom of the stairs, where I stopped and turned around to face him. "So, my mother's up there, lying in wait like a shark. In case you didn't notice, she was watching from the window."

He looked up toward the window. "Well, she can't see us at this angle," he said, taking a step closer and putting an arm around my waist. He pulled me closer then wrapped another arm around my waist. Closer still, slowly, waiting to see if I'd object. I did not. "Will I see you again?" he asked softly, just before his lips connected with mine. I moaned my response, and in my head said yes, oh yes. The tip of his tongue touched mine and my hands, which had been up against his chest, snaked around his neck. He, too, moaned a response and pulled me even closer. And then it happened.

"Amalia! *Hol vagy*? Translation: Where are you? We leapt away from each other as though we were teenagers.

"I'll be right there, Mom. Go back inside before you catch a cold," I snapped in English, for Matt's benefit. I heard the door close but knew not to waste time or to assume that she'd gone inside.

"Give me a call when you have a chance and we'll make

plans then," I suggested. Then added, "She'll be back out in two minutes, or she could still be standing there listening!" He drew me close for a split second and gave me another quick kiss then reminded me that he only had my work number. I told him I'd call him and hurried up the stairs.

As I reached the top, I remembered my manners and shouted "Thank you" as I turned around. He was still standing at the bottom of the stairs, looking at me, smiling. I grinned back and then quickly went inside to face the beady eyes.

And there they were, looking at me, expectantly. My mother nodded approval and commented that I was home at a respectable time. I feigned a headache, telling them to stay up as late as they wanted but that I had to get to bed as I had a busy day ahead. I wished them a hasty goodnight, gave them a peck on the cheek and slithered off to the sanctity of my room where I reran my mental videotape of Matt's kiss a dozen times. Lips still tingling, I started to doze off with a smile...

And then shot upright in a flash, my eyes flying open in realization. He had lied to me!

CHAPTER THIRTEEN

*S*tupid, stupid, stupid! How could I not have picked up on it? Joey could not have been Matt's childhood friend. The man was obviously too old to have gone to school with Matt. Why had Matt lied to me? Was he guarding me? Or was he guarding a secret? Had he seen me driving back and forth in front of Joey's house? Was he dating me just to find out what I knew about the murders? And the person that he'd hinted was watching us in the restaurant, was that meant to make me paranoid so that I'd be sure to keep him around? He obviously knew Joey, and he'd also been here on New Years' Eve. Was this really a coincidence? Something didn't jive here. Maybe Matt was the one I should be careful around. I had been patient, trusting that the police were doing their job, but my patience was wearing thin. Tomorrow I'd figure things out.

I slept fitfully and gave up completely by 8:00 a.m. when I heard my parents moving about. Of course, The Aliens! Somehow I had forgotten they were there, and that meant I couldn't even lounge around in bed. My morning routine disrupted, I stomped into the kitchen, grunted hello, and started the coffee.

I glared at the pot, willing it to brew faster. I couldn't jibber-jabber in Hungarian with no java and too little sleep. Never in tune with my moods, my parents were clueless and tried to engage me in conversation.

How was the date? Grunt. Will you be seeing him again? Snort. I could almost hear the rustle of their bushy eyebrows as they rose behind me. I hurriedly grabbed a cup, yanked the pot, filled quickly and returned the pot to continue the drip cycle. Milk. Sugar. More sugar. More sugar. Sip. Brain cells activating. Houston, we have lift-off!

I turned, forcing a bright smile. "Everything's fine. I'm just not a morning person. Let me make you some breakfast so that you're all set when the agent gets here. I can't join you for the house search but I'll give you a set of keys to the house so you can come and go as you please." I prayed that Janet remembered to show them properties a good thirty minutes or more away.

"But we thought you were coming with us," my dad said. "You're not open today, right? We were hoping to get your opinion."

"Not open, but I still have a lot to do. I have a special event next week so I have to create some promotional flyers and deliver them. We'll be hosting a Murder Mystery Dinner." Not knowing what this was, I explained to them how a cast comes in and serves the customers while acting out a skit. One by one, cast members are killed off, and by the end of the meal, the murderer is revealed.

Seeing as how everyone in the community was quite fascinated by the real-life murders that had taken place, I was fairly certain this event would be a big hit but, only if I got the word out. That meant I had to post flyers and stuff mailboxes.

My father's reaction was typical: "That's stupid. Why would anyone come to something like that and pay you money?"

"It's actually a lot of fun," I replied. "I've been to one before, and it's very entertaining, plus you get a great meal.

I can make a lot of money from this event."

He wasn't convinced, but then again, if it didn't involve becoming an accountant, he wasn't impressed. I no longer took it personally.

Speaking of murders, this was the perfect opportunity to ease into the details of recent events, and I was just opening my mouth to tell them when the real estate agent arrived. It would have to wait.

"See you later," I chirped, "and remember, Ottawa's pretty big, so keep an open mind!" I shot Janet a last meaningful look and she winked in return. While my parents were putting on their winter gear, I said softly, so only she could hear, "Please, don't tell them about the murders, they don't know yet." She nodded.

"I have some great properties to show you, Mr. and Mrs. Kis, I'm sure we'll find something you like." With that, they were gone. I grabbed another cup of coffee and snuggled in bed to unwind with a cooking show and a pad of paper to jot down ideas. I did some of my best thinking while watching other people cook.

So, where to begin? Do I call Matt and confront him about the lie? Do I play along and try to pump him for information? That might be risky, and of course there could be a reasonable explanation, too, but I couldn't think of one. I pushed these thoughts aside for a while and worked on my flyer for the Murder Mystery Dinner.

Once finished, I printed off dozens of copies, and headed out to post and distribute the flyers. Outside, near the bottom of the steps, I noticed a black object embedded in the snow. I approached cautiously, just in case it was a skunk. It wasn't moving, so I edged closer and discovered that it was Matt's hat, dropped and forgotten in our moment of passion. Or pretend passion. Could he really fake that though? My mind laughed back at me. Sure, if he was a killer...

I picked it up and threw it in the backseat of my car. Next, I headed to the corner store just a minute's drive away and posted the flyer on the bulletin board inside the store. Then I headed over to the liquor store.

I picked up a bottle of raspberry vodka since I was running low. I couldn't risk running out with my parents over and having to deal with them. I then asked the guy at the cash register if I could post my flyer somewhere since they didn't have a bulletin board. As he was reading it over, he started to shift nervously.

"I'm sorry lady, I'd love to help you out..."

"But...." I prodded, wondering what reason he could possibly have.

"Well, Mr. Leonardo is one of our very good customers. I don't want to end up on his bad side." He looked at me apologetically.

"I see," I replied, even though I didn't see at all. I was getting a pretty good idea though that Leonardo had his thumb on this town.

I stormed off with my vodka and I went around to the various subdivisions, posting flyers on mailboxes. In this neighborhood, as was the case in many others in Ottawa, residents did not have mailboxes at their house but had to collect their mail at a designated area (normally on the corner of their street) where each person had a key for their mail slot. The exception was the main road. There houses did have their own mailboxes, and as I stuffed flyers into them, an idea took shape. I was nearing Joey's old house and my brain cells were now fully awake and buzzing with excitement.

As I drove past, I saw a small black car in the laneway and quickly made up my mind. Checking behind me, the coast was clear for a quick U-turn. Then, drawing a deep breath, I quickly turned left onto the driveway. The fence was closed, so I couldn't pull up close.

Leaving the car on the road, I scooted through the bars of the fence that was meant to keep people like me out. I tried to ignore all the junk that was piled up outside as I made my way to the front door of the Hoarder House, as it was known in the neighborhood. There was no doorbell, so I knocked tentatively. After a minute, I screwed up my courage and knocked louder.

"Yes?" A behemoth of a woman opened the door and peered out suspiciously. She was very tall, likely at least six feet with chin length stringy brown (not caramel) hair and an Adam's apple bigger than her boobs. She looked to be about my age, but there was no effort at trying to maximize any good features that may have been lying latent under her pasty skin.

"I'm really sorry to bother you at your time of loss, but Matt forgot his hat at my house and I don't have his number. He mentioned that he was close friends with Joey, so I was hoping that perhaps you knew of a way to give this to him?" Smooth. Yes, great line. I congratulated myself.

She looked confused. "You must be mistaken, but yes, I can ask Joey to give it to Matt the next time they get together."

It was my turn to be confused. She was talking in the present tense. I had to tread lightly. Perhaps explaining who I was might clear things up. "My name is Amalia and I own the Whine and Cheese bistro that just opened not long ago".

She did not react, nor did she say anything to prompt me. I pressed on. "Are you Joey's daughter, or a relative?"

She laughed oddly, "Oh, no, he's my boyfriend! My name is Eunice." Again, the present tense. And a girlfriend? There had to be a good twenty years age difference between them.

"Please accept my condolences. I don't mean to intrude. Perhaps I have the wrong house. I'm talking about a Joey who had rather long, grayish hair, maybe about fifty years old..."

I got that odd laugh again that made me cringe. "You have the right house, that's Joey, but he's actually thirty-two." She glanced nervously behind her. "Come on in," she said hesitantly and motioned me inside while she continued to speak. "Don't mind the mess. Joey went prematurely gray in his early twenties. You keep apologizing...did something happen?" She looked at me suspiciously.

I looked around and noticed a number of empty boxes and a few that looked to be in the process of being packed. Everywhere I looked though, there was stuff on top of stuff and more stuff. She noticed my glance and explained.

"I've been helping Joey pack up some of this stuff to get rid of it. He never did get around to it after his parents died, and the piles just keep growing. He's ready for a change. I think he should be home soon, if you want to wait for him." She said this merely to be polite, as the smile she offered did not quite reach her eyes.

Suddenly two very important things shot through my brain: first, Matt was telling the truth, he had grown up with Joey since they were the same age; and second, this lady did not seem to know what had happened to her boyfriend.

Do I tell her? Hell no!

Shaking my head, I started babbling, "You know, I must have misunderstood something. To be honest, it was my first date with Matt and I was so nervous that honestly, his lips moved and I really didn't hear anything. I'm really sorry to take up your time. I'll just leave the hat. Thank you so much for helping me out."

"Okay, no problem. I hope it works out. I haven't known Matt that long since I've only been dating Joey about four months now, but he seems really nice. From what Joey's told me, he hasn't dated much in a couple of years. You'll both have to stop by one day." She towered over me as she walked me to the door, a little too close for my comfort. Maybe it was just the place that was making me feel claustrophobic.

"Sure, that sounds great," I smiled, and then bolted to my car, barely able to turn away in time to conceal the tears welling in my eyes.

Driving back to my house, I angrily wiped at the tears now flowing freely down my cheeks. The poor girl had no clue. How she couldn't know was bizarre, but she had no clue that her boyfriend had been killed. What if she was in danger?

I quickly parked the car and ran upstairs. Frantically, I called Matt and got his voicemail. By now I was definitely sniveling.

"Matt, it's Amalia. You have to go to Joey's house as soon as possible. His girlfriend is there and she doesn't know he's dead. I'll explain later." I left him my cell number and hung up, ashamed, knowing I'd have to explain why I was there and hoping he'd understand.

I brewed another pot of coffee and paced the house, practicing what I'd say to Matt, trying to find a way of putting a different spin on it but coming up with nothing plausible and scolding myself for my Inspector Clouseau detective skills.

But I did find out that Matt had not lied, and since Eunice thought Joey was alive, then obviously she couldn't be his killer. That narrowed the suspect list down by two people.

That prompted me to stop pacing and whip out my note pad and sit down on the couch to write a suspect list. I tapped my pen a while. I couldn't think while sitting, so I started pacing again. I returned to the note pad. Stared at it a while. And then a germ of an idea formed.

Yes, that's it! Don't let that idea slip away, I muttered aloud to myself. First, I was pretty sure both murders were connected. I had told the police that I may have seen someone who looked like the second victim in the bistro on New Year's Eve. I tried to think back to the features that I'd caught only a glimpse of but came up with nothing. Perhaps Nicole or Nora remembered him. We'd never thought to compare notes. I quickly called Nicole.

"Nic, the guy who was killed—do you remember if he

was at our party in the bistro on New Year's Eve?"

"I don't remember seeing him, but it was super busy and I did spend some time on stage too, so I wasn't serving the customers as much as you and Nora were."

"Okay, I'll call you later—oh, and Matt kissed me! And my parents are visiting and are looking for a house to move here—remind me to tell you all this when we talk later." I hung up as I heard her screeching for me to wait, and dialed Nora's number.

We caught up for a few moments, not having seen each other since the night of the NYE party. I posed the same question to her that I had to Nicole. I knew the cops had called her to take her statement, but other than a quick call from her to see how I was holding up, there hadn't been much to discuss about the murder at the time.

"You know, now that I think about it, I do remember something that was a bit odd that night. Remember that table you asked me to take over for you because the guys were creeping you out a bit? Two of the guys were pretty quiet, but one in particular barely said a word. He didn't look like he belonged with the others. Mostly, the other two did all the talking, and he just kind of sat there looking nervous. Come to think of it, none of them looked like they were out for a party."

"That's right Nora, you're brilliant! The guys in the jeans and black t-shirts!. I think you're on to something because the guy on the stairs had on those same clothes."

"What made you think of calling me to see what I remember?" Nora asked.

"Well, I haven't heard anything about the case, so I'm thinking I might start snooping around a bit." I didn't mention that I had already snooped a little here and there.

"Oh, that sounds like fun!" Nora exclaimed to my surprise. "If you need a hand snooping, let me know. It'll get me out of the house. The man's driving me bananas!"

We hung up and I dashed down to the bistro with my notepad. Thumbing through the reservation book, I found the entries for New Years' Eve. That would be a good starting point. I'd call everyone who made a reservation to see if I could flush something out.

But what line could I use? I practiced: "Yes, hello, you lost a body at my bistro..." Okay, maybe that wouldn't be the best tactic.

I added the names and phone numbers to my list of suspects but had to put my plans on hold as my cell phone rang. Call display: Matt.

Showtime!

CHAPTER FOURTEEN

"*Hi* Matt, thanks for calling me back. I had a really nice time last night, by the way." Better say that while I had the chance.

"What happened? Are you okay? You sounded almost hysterical on the phone. And I had a nice time too." His voice softened and I could almost hear a smile over the lines.

"I'll make a long but embarrassing story short, Matt, because I prefer to tell you part of it in person, but I ended up at Joey's house and his girlfriend Eunice was there. I'm not sure how this is even possible, but she seemed to think Joey is still alive. I almost told her—me, a complete stranger, can you imagine? You have to get over there to let her know! What if she's in danger?"

There was a sharp intake of breath. "That's actually not that surprising. They haven't been dating too long, and I remember she'd made plans to go to the states to visit some family before she'd ever met Joey. She must have just gotten back to town and is at his house waiting for him to get home, thinking he's just out running errands. The cops have been waiting for her return. No one knew her last name so they couldn't track her down. I'll go to see her now, but then I'll come by your place to get the rest of the story. I'm sure curious as to why you were there in the first place."

We hung up and I breathed a sigh of relief. Okay, that went well, hopefully he wouldn't think I was an idiot when he found out the rest.

I went back upstairs and paced. I freshened my make-up, which is really just some green or gray eyeliner on the top lid and a swipe of mascara. I gave up on lipstick years ago, succumbing instead to my lip balm addiction. I straightened my hair and spritzed on some lemon sugar and coconut Victoria's Secret body spray. I plucked a gray hair that had materialized out of nowhere. I prayed my parents wouldn't return before I had a chance to talk with Matt. In fact, I blamed my parents for the gray hair.

I broke a world record rushing to the door when the bell rang, but screeched to a halt when I peered out through the peephole and saw the Kramer hair standing at attention.

Which reminds me, I haven't had the opportunity to describe my parents yet. This will be a treat.

Once upon a time, there had been a TV show called *Seinfeld*. The main character, Jerry Seinfeld, had a friend named Kramer who had a crazy crop of hair. My dad was no doubt the inspiration. The rest of dad, however, resembled a barrel with scrawny chicken-type limbs.

My mom wore her short, dyed, dark brown hair pinned back with bobby pins and sported an extra fifty pounds on her short frame. Big glasses magnified her eyeballs and gave her an owlish appearance. Both dressed in a style popular three decades earlier. They weren't ugly people, but with one look, you could tell they were different and not of Canadian decent.

"Why didn't you use the keys?" I asked.

"You have so many locks, we didn't know where to begin. It's a good thing you were home; we would have been standing out there all day. What's with all these locks, anyway?"

I almost laughed out loud, since their house was like Fort Knox. I stifled the giggle and decided it was time to tell them about the murders. I had my mouth open and then the doorbell rang again. This time it was Matt, looking drained. I muttered a quick 'see you later' to my parents, grabbed my keys off the entryway table and shot out the door.

"Let's go to the bistro and talk there," I told Matt, while grabbing his hand and leading him to the rear entrance. I settled him in a cozy chair and told him I'd be right back. Soon, two cups of coffee laced with Baileys sat between us on a small table.

"You were right," he said dejectedly. "She didn't know yet. She was speechless. I'm sure she was in shock because she just shut down, didn't show any emotion. She mentioned that she knew, since he was a hoarder, that he likely had some issues, but she said that lately he'd been getting some professional help, both mentally and to help him start sorting through everything in the house, which he was also letting her help him with. She was hoping it was because they were in love and that he was trying to make room in his house for her.

"She couldn't think of a single person that would want to kill him though, and didn't know of any friends other than me and his cousins that he'd sometimes see. She had no clue what he'd been up to as she'd been out of town the last few weeks, in the States. He has a land-line but no cell phone, so they couldn't text and didn't talk because her long distance cell bill would have been huge.

"Funny thing though..." his voice trailed off, then he looked at me curiously, "...she gave me the hat I was wearing last night before I left. Said you had left it with her to give to me, claiming you didn't have my number."

I turned pink. Beat red. Okay, purple. Taking a big swig of my coffee for strength, I sighed, and keeping my eyes on the ground, mumbled my apology. "Listen, I'm really sorry. This is the embarrassing part I alluded to earlier. I couldn't sleep last night, kept tossing and turning because something just wasn't making sense. By the time I got up this morning, I was convinced that you might be the killer, so when I saw a car in the driveway at Joeys, I got this crazy idea to snoop for information. And while I was there, I found out the missing piece of the puzzle that had been bothering me and which made me realize you're not the killer..." I finally screwed up the nerve to take a peek at him from behind my curtain of hair. He raised a brow, with a 'go on' look. His mouth was a thin little angry line, like something out of a cartoon drawing.

"See, the thing is, you had said you were childhood friends and went to school together, but all I really knew about him was that he had gray hair. So I assumed that he was at least fifty or older and it was impossible that you went to school together and maybe you killed him and were just hanging out with me to keep tabs on what I'd learn from the cops. But then I found out he went prematurely gray and that he was your age and maybe..."

"Yes?"

"Well, maybe you really did like me and that's why you'd been hanging out with me." My voice was barely more than a whisper and my eyes fixated again on the floor.

I felt movement but dared not to look up. If he was leaving, I didn't want to see it, but I would understand. I had clearly shown a complete lack of trust and although it was because I was spooked by recent events, it was still not a good way to start off a relationship.

Leaning forward, he cradled me in his arms and held me without saying a word. The heat radiated between our bodies, and I felt my face go purple once again. Hell, I think my whole damn body went purple! Finally, he kissed me gently on the forehead. the nose and the chin. Feathery kisses from the chin to the corner of my mouth. On the mouth, his tongue teased my own in a silent dance. Hello, it said. Let's tango.

He pulled away a fraction of an inch, only enough to whisper in my ear, "Yes, I do really like you." My hair stirred slightly from his breath and made me shiver.

We remained like that a few more moments. This time, I angled my head to whisper in his ear. "I'm sorry. I hope you can understand." He gave me a quick peck on the nose and dragged me to my feet, proceeding to give me a bear hug, lightening the mood. "What's a guy got to do to get some grub around here, anyway?" he joked.

Phew, I thought. I didn't screw things up. But it was his own fault. He should have told me about Joey's hair. So for that, a little punishment was in order. An evening with my parents would be perfect.

"You're right; stay for dinner. I have to cook for my parents anyway, and they'll be wondering what we're doing down here. In fact, I'm almost surprised that they're not down here, pounding on the door and wondering what's going on. Too many areas where we could get naughty down here, you know?" I winked and both his eyebrows shot up in surprise. Growling, he made a lunge in my direction but I slipped away and started gathering supplies that I would need from the kitchen.

"Alright, brace yourself, this isn't going to be pleasant, but if you have any intentions of dating me, you may as well get to know The Aliens, so let's go." And back up the stairs we went.

CHAPTER FIFTEEN

My parents were sitting on the couch watching Dr. Oz on TV. I announced that Matt would be staying for dinner and that I was going to start cooking.

"Hallo, Mutt; so, my daughter not scaring you away, eh?" my dad said while chuckling. Good Lord, I may have to kill him.

Matt threw back his head and laughed, clearly amused. "No, sir, we had a lovely dinner last night. Hopefully I'll be seeing lots of your daughter. How did the house searching go today?"

"Oh, very good, ya! That lady, she taking us evry vare, so far away from Amalia. So I show her picture I get from paper here at house and I say to her to taking me to this house in picture. Ve maybe buying." He pulled out a page from the local paper in Robin and my heart froze. NO! Hell no!

But oh yes! Yes, indeed. To my horror, the picture from the real estate section of the local paper showed a house a mere few minutes' drive from my house. My coffee-jazzed brain shifted into high gear.

"Oh, boy, you don't want to live out here at your age!

There's no city sewer system here, so you have to worry about a septic tank, and there's no city water, so you have your own well and water softener system to worry about; it's a real pain sometimes. And, oh wow, the land out this way is all half an acre or more; you'll be spending the whole day mowing the lawn, and that would be a lot of work for mum...you can't do it because of your bad knee, Dad."

"Oh sure, Mama can do; ve buying grass tractor if ve getting house, or ve get teenager to cutting grass".

I was screwed. Seemed to me they'd already made up their minds.

I went about preparing the meal while they resumed watching TV. Matt kept me company in the kitchen, sitting at the small island on one of the bar stools. I poured us each a hefty glass of red wine labeled WTF and brought my parents a glass as well. May as well get bombed and dull the pain.

Luckily my parents kept to themselves, engrossed in the television. I sent Dr. Oz a silent thank you for keeping their attention focused on something other than me. I brought out the plates and utensils and Matt transported them to the dining area to set the small table. Room for four comfortably, or a tight fit for six. I wasn't sure if it was the glow from the wine, but my house was feeling very cozy. I knew I could get used to Matt puttering around with me.

Dinner was ready. I had made a Hungarian Goulash, served with a crusty sour dough bread. We gathered around the table and ate in silence for a few minutes. Then the inevitable...

"You go to Hungary, you learn to making the Goulash." My mother: she doesn't say much in English, the language is difficult for her. She had moved here at the age of thirty, my age now, my parents' marriage being the second for each. Although she had worked in Hungary, she had never worked outside the home in Canada and was shy when it came to speaking.

"I know how to making Goulash; I don't needing to go to Hungary for that." There it was; I was speaking like them now. Matt looked at me in surprise. I shrugged. I had no explanation, something weird happens when I'm around my folks.

"But you can making better. Is good, but is not like in Hungary."

"That's because I don't use congealed pig fat," I snapped.

Matt came to my rescue: "I love it! I've never had it before, and I really like the paprika spice." I shot him a thank you look. He decided to come to my rescue again. "Why are you moving to Ottawa?" he asked my parents.

"You know, lots of politicka in Quebec, and ve don't speak the French. And ve vorry about Amalia here alone all the time."

"Oh, you don't have to worry, I've been keeping my eye on Mali since the murders, making sure she's safe and that no one's hanging around."

I gasped. He hadn't! Oh yes, he had. He'd spilled the beans before I'd had a chance to say anything.

An uncomfortable silence followed and Matt shot me questioning look. I gave my head a slight shake, my eyes bulging. Slowly, the English translated to Hungarian in their heads while I waited with dread. I took a fortifying chug of wine.

"Vat you mean, murderz?" my father finally sputtered.

I quickly filled them in, downplaying everything, emphasizing the likelihood of it all being completely random, each a one-time occurrence. The police were working very hard on solving the case and were concerned about my safety. "Even though they were certain nothing would happen again, Matt is here to make sure I am safe. That's how we met."

Okay, so it wasn't completely true, but it wasn't completely a lie either. I had learned many years ago that withholding information from my parents was my only hope for being able to lead any type of independent life. And the best way to lie was to base it on some truth. Everyone knew that.

They didn't look happy but there was a sudden renewed interest in Matt, even though he wasn't Hungarian, for which he would never be forgiven.

"So, Mutt, you security guard?" my dad asked bluntly.

"Well, sir, I was a police officer for a few years. Now I own my own company which provides security guards and has private investigation services, called Secure n' Snoop"". I dropped my fork. Owns his own company?

This time my dad was definitely interested. "Vy you stop being cop?"

"I did it for a few years. I guess I saw too many things that I couldn't do much about. When my partner was shot, I knew it was time to change jobs. Luckily he survived; he works for me now." I suspected that he was talking about Ricky.

While they chatted, I sulked over the prospect of my parents moving close by and envisioned them popping by each day and telling me that my cooking wasn't quite Hungarian enough, among many, many other things...

As the conversation died down, we cleared the table and Matt helped me with the dishes while my parents took showers, preparing for an early bedtime. They were meeting with the realtor again the next morning for a second look at the house around the corner as well as some other potentials—unfortunately, all properties close to mine. I made a mental note never to do business with Janet again—after I pried more information out of her, of course.

Matt and I sat on the couch, Hummer squarely in the middle of us, better than any chastity belt at ensuring we kept our distance. I was the first to speak. "Ricky?"

"We didn't think he'd survive, but he's a tough one. He was determined—he had reason to be. He'd just met his girlfriend; four years later, they're still madly in love."

I was kind of impressed: Four years and still full of passion. That was something.

Matt reached around the cat, despite a warning growl, and took my hand in his, stroking the top with his thumb. "It's been quite a day, hasn't it?" he asked softly.

"Not all of it bad," I grinned.

Reluctantly he rose, having to return home for an early morning at work the next day. Although he was still technically on vacation, an urgent matter had called him into the office. He did promise to be back in a few hours to make sure everything was okay, and he wanted to check on Joey's girlfriend again on his way home. He'd have to go home, catch a few z's, come out here, and then get back home for more shut-eye.

To thank him, I gave him a smoldering kiss that ended with one of his hands reaching under my shirt and the other cupping my behind before I leaped away, certain my parents would come out of the spare room any moment. I admit, I looked guilty, having reverted back to "child" status, rather than grown-up, with my parents under my roof.

A final kiss and he was on his way.

I blew out a deep sigh. It had been close to two years since my last romp with anyone. I was impressed with myself that I hadn't tackled him and dragged him to my room. Had my parents not been there, I might have.

The next morning consisted of a rushed breakfast and tossing my folks out the door. I watched my morning food shows, googled Secure n' Snoop and impatiently waited until 11:00 a.m. before calling anyone. Then I took out my suspect list.

The first person I called had a local number and a not-so-friendly answering machine message that advised me, "I'm not here, you know what to do." At the beep, I explained who I was and that I was looking for anyone who may have known the man murdered at my bistro so that I may offer my condolences and a free meal. I figured the "free" aspect might hook someone into coming in, and then I could pump them for information.

The second had neither an answering service nor a response. Who doesn't have voicemail in this day and age?

I went through the list, mostly leaving messages and connecting with a handful of people and presenting my spiel. No one took the bait, but everyone seemed willing to gossip and offer speculation.

"Did you happen to see anything interesting or out of the ordinary that night?" I prodded one gabby lady.

"Well, there was a group of men at the table next to us bickering most of the night," she offered. "Seems they kept arguing about how they should have bought a place rather than having waited. I could be mistaken, but it sounded like they meant your place, and they kept watching you. You are the very tall lady there, right?"

My heart skipped a beat. "Yes, that would be me. Do you recall what they looked like?"

She started to laugh. "No, I'm sorry. I 'd had a bit too much to drink and everyone looked pretty fuzzy to me that night. I only remembered this because they were such downers."

I jotted down the information. So, someone else was interested in my property. Was I sitting on a goldmine? Oil? Diamonds?

Once done, I crawled back into my warm bed and called Nicole so that we finally had a chance to catch up on every juicy detail, butt grabs included.

"Did Officer Sean say anything about the murders? Any progress, ideas, anything?" I prodded, once our giggles had died down.

"I don't usually see him for long, but anything he's mentioned, we already know. You should call him for an update; I'm sure he wouldn't mind. If he mentions anything about me, just say that you and I are hanging out, okay? I've been talking to this other guy online for months now and he seems really interesting. Tonight is my second date with him. But after this guy, I'll definitely take a break. Maybe it'll work out with him...or Sean." She gave me Sean's work number and extension.

I pondered my next move as I got out of bed and puttered about, tidying up. I cleaned the litter box, started a load of laundry and passed the vacuum quickly over the area rugs. I made a grocery list and composed a list of questions to ask Officer Sean. There was just something about him that was off-putting.

Finally ready, I reached for my cell phone, only to realize it needed charging. I plugged it in then went down to the bistro to use the landline as it occurred to me that our reservation book might come in useful to the police.

Voicemail: I left a message, mentioning the reservation book but neglecting to mention my earlier activities. As I hung up, something caught my eye. As usual, the blinds were closed, but a shadow seemed to have passed by. I froze, fumbled for my cell to call Matt, and realized it was upstairs. I didn't know his number by heart yet to call from the landline. With speed dial on cell phones, who knew anyone's number anymore?

I rifled through the reservation book for his number but another shadow distracted me and I abandoned the search as I shot across the room and flattened myself against the wall next to the blinds. I listened carefully, heard the soft scuffle of feet outside. Panic froze me to the spot while my brain screamed at me to move. While the blood pounded in my ears, I saw, rather than heard, the door knob jiggle ever so slightly as someone from the outside tried the handle. I searched my mind. Did my parents take the keys? Maybe they were back and trying to get in through this door for some reason. I forced myself to peak out of the corner of the blind, ever so slowly, so as not to attract attention. From this angle I saw nothing. I moved the blind just a little more, and then the world shattered. I jumped back a split second before all hell broke loose, tripping over one of the chairs and landing on my back. As I went down, my head hit the corner of one of the side tables. My last memory was of splintered glass.

CHAPTER SIXTEEN

*H*ours later, I opened my eyes to the unsettling sight of six beady eyeballs staring at me. The startling green ones crinkled up in a smile, but with undertones of worry. The two sets of brown ones did not smile. I tried to sit up and felt my mother's beefy hand shoot out and restrain me. "*Nem,*" she said. No.

The fragmented memories came back with a jolt as I realized I was in a hospital bed. "My head," I groaned.

"Yep, back of your noggin," Matt replied. "You were out cold. Your parents had just come back from house hunting and saw someone tall bundled up in winter gear smash out your window with a bat and then go running toward the back. He probably took off through the trails. The cops don't think he actually hurt you. It seems you did this to yourself."

"My face?" I have already established that I can be vain.

"Your face is fine. When the window was smashed, the blinds prevented most of the glass from flying in at you."

"Vat the hell you get youself into, Amalia?" my father barked, only to have my mum tell him in Hungarian to save it for later. She was usually rather submissive, but at times she would surprise me. And when she took control, oh boy, watch out.

She stroked the hair back from my forehead—something I'd always hated since I did not like how I looked without bangs—yet I was equally annoyed and comforted, and annoyed that it comforted me. Yes, no surprise, vanity won out, as I brushed my bangs back into place. I couldn't have Matt see me without bangs!

My mum talked Dad into leaving me with Matt so that they could go take care of the window for me. They had left it with a board in place but I was supposed to be open for business later that night. My Thursday opening would have to be postponed, but hopefully everything would be in order for the next day.

I thanked them, for once grateful that they were there, and Matt assured them he'd drive me home once the doctor released me.

"Okay, give it to me. I checked your website so in addition to having been a cop, I know you're also a skilled private investigator and you already told me that you have worked in security. What are your thoughts about all this?" I pinned Matt with a no nonsense stare. With his background, I knew he knew more than he was letting on.

He assessed me for a few minutes, wondering how he should word his answer. "Don't sugar-coat it, Matt; spill it. All this has been dragging on for weeks, and it's getting worse instead of better." He nodded once and began.

"Okay, here's what I figure. I'm sure the two murders are linked. You've either done something to piss the murderer off, without knowing it, or he thinks you heard or saw something, or he's lost something at the bistro that could tie everything to him. Otherwise, he wouldn't be watching you, throwing rocks to intimidate you, following us to the restaurant or breaking in your window." He studied my face, saw no signs of hysteria, and forged ahead.

"And, we don't know what his intentions were when he

broke your window, since he was scared off. What you said to your parents the other night wasn't a lie, really. After we were followed, I contacted Officer Sean to let him know. I used to work with him; he's a good guy. Doesn't talk much; he's the analytical type, you know. There haven't been many clues in this case, but he did mention that there's been a string of break-ins around here lately that may all be tied together. There's nothing linking Joey to anyone, no enemies that they could trace. They spoke to his girlfriend yesterday after I had gone to see her—I called Sean to let her know she was in town. She couldn't think of anyone he's had problems with, but they're putting a trace on his cousins just to be sure."

"Did Joey have a big family?"

"No, just a couple of cousins actually, and his parents were both killed in a car crash when he was only seventeen. He lived with an aunt and uncle after that, until he was old enough to move out on his own, into his late parents' home, where he is now. Or rather, was..." Sadness flickered across his face for a moment. I was reaching toward him when the doctor walked into the room.

"What day is it, Ms. Kis?" Pronounced 'Kiss', which is what I was hoping to get before he waltzed in.

"Thursday?"

"What happened to you?"

I recounted, briefly, the events.

"How old are you?"

"Thirty." Passing the test, I got the 'get out of jail free' card. I was being released but with strict conditions.

Looking at Matt, the doctor gave instructions to keep ice packs on my head for twenty minute intervals, but not to apply pressure. Wake me every two to three hours, asking me the questions he'd just asked. If I didn't wake up, or forgot details, or if I vomited repeatedly, then call an ambulance immediately. And I should get lots of rest in a dark room. Tylenol as needed. No alcohol. No exercise, nothing physical. His eyes bore into Matt. He colored slightly, getting the drift: no sex. That's okay; our relationship wasn't quite there yet anyway.

I got out of the hospital bed slowly, fighting off a sudden ripple of nausea. My head felt bruised and tender and I couldn't wait to be in my own bed. Seeing me blanch, Matt told me to just stay sitting on the bed then went off in search of a wheelchair.

He wheeled me to the hospital entrance with instructions to wait while he got his car. Minutes later he was back and helped me into the passenger seat. Both of our breaths caught slightly in our throats as his hand grazed my breast while fastening my seat belt. "Sorry," he mumbled, grinning.

Pain and nerves make me babble. I giggled. "Any excuse to cop a feel?" He kissed me gently and whispered, "I already copped a feel last night, remember? And I didn't need any excuses." I blushed my usual choice of purple.

The ride home lasted about thirty minutes to an eternity. We caught the tail end of traffic, with just a bit of stop and go on the Queensway Highway #417 heading into Robin.

"Do you have Tylenol at home?" Matt questioned.

"Yes." It was all I could manage, as a wave of nausea made the back of my tongue quiver like jelly.

At home, my parents were waiting anxiously on the couch. As Matt supported my weight with an arm around my waist and my arm around his neck, my mother rushed forward and grabbed me from the other side, murmuring Hungarian pet names she used to call me when I was a little girl. "Little angel. Sweet little bug."

They ushered me into bed and then after a moment Matt reappeared with a tall glass of juice, a bottle of water and a bottle of Tylenol. My mother brought a plate of fried veal schnitzel—my second favorite, with first place going to her fried chicken.

The thought of food turned my stomach, but in the end the schnitzel won. I was weak, I was no match for the schnitzel, and of course I hadn't eaten since breakfast. Since I refused to fry food, it was a real treat, and one that I would enjoy guilt free any time my mom would make it.

My dad hovered in the doorway then came and sat on the edge of my bed, just looking at me, shaking his head. I reached over and patted his hand. I may have promised to take an accounting course, I can't recall. At that moment all I wanted to do was take a nap.

A few minutes later, Matt was asking me my name. Or had it been two hours already? "Amalia Kis. I know you say 'Kiss', but it's actually pronounced like a "quiche" in Hungarian. It means small. Amalia means work. I'm thirty years old. Someone tried to take me out with a bat today. Can I go back to sleep now?"

With that I rolled over and returned to sleep. He poked me.

"What's your name?"

Holy heck, we just did this, didn't we?

"You've slept for another two hours already. What's your name?"

Same spiel. Amalia Kis, blah-blah-blah. I had a few questions of my own.

"What time is it?"

"It's eleven at night."

It was obviously going to be a long night. I drank some juice, closed my eyes, and then opened them. "You're still here? Are you hanging out with my parents?"

He chuckled. "Yeah, actually, I am. Go back to sleep; everything's fine here.

I clocked out after "yeah", the rest sounding very far away as I drifted off. At one a.m. I was awakened by the feeling of my bangs being swept off my forehead. Mom: the same conversation, but this time in Hungarian. This was a bit more difficult, but not due to the concussion. The Hungarian gerbil just wasn't on the wheel after being woke from a deep sleep, but I muddled through.

I assumed Matt had left but didn't have the energy to

ask. I mumbled that I loved her and asked if it was time for more Tylenol. "Not yet," she said, but replaced my ice pack.

Later, Dad: more Hungarian and a precious gift of Tylenol.

Next I woke to the feeling of sandpaper on my arm. Managing to pry one lid open I saw a look of concern on Hummer's face. He settled down in the space between my knees and my butt. He was brave. I slumbered again.

I no longer knew the time nor did I care. I awoke to little feather light brush strokes on my face. I tried to place the sensation through my fog. A stroke rested on my lips and I recognized his subtle scent. My eyes flew open.

"What are you still doing here? It must be really late by now."

"I've been sleeping on the couch since your parents insisted that I stay. I think they were worried the guy would come back. How old are you?"

Ah, yes: the concussion test.

"Old enough to have someone I'm dating in my bed." I couldn't resist. I was warm and snuggly and he was just so damn hot in the soft glow of light. He smiled and lay next to me for few moments, stroking my hair. Not the way my mother does. I wanted so much to stay awake and enjoy it, but as much as I fought it, I drifted away again.

He continued to check on me for the remainder of the night, or rather, morning, having assured my parents he'd keep watch and insisting that they sleep. If he thought this was a good opportunity for him to prove his worth to them, he was absolutely correct.

Just before six in the morning I awoke on my own and was pleasantly surprised to still find him by my side. I guessed that after he last checked on me, he'd dozed off. I studied him in the glow of the small bedside lamp. I reached over and gently placed my hand on his chest. A few moments later, I slowly moved my hand to his face, tracing a cheekbone with my finger to wake him.

Opening an eye, he looked at me. "What's your name?" I asked him.

"Funny girl, are you? I take it you're feeling better."

Oh yes, I sure was. I lifted myself on one elbow to get a better look at him then grimaced as my head splintered in pain. I quickly sagged back against the pillows. "Tylenol," I croaked.

Juice and Tylenol in hand, he gently helped me to a sitting position and put the pills in my mouth. He lifted the glass to my lips and I drank until it was empty. I was thirsty and needed the strength of meat. "Schnitzel?" I asked hopefully, knowing my mother always made extra.

He returned with a schnitzel for each of us and I patted the bed by my side. He shook his head no. "Your parents might get up any time now. I'm not going to take that risk and have your dad shoot me."

"Don't worry. He'd just attack you with his hands," I reassured him, grinning.

We munched in silenced, enjoying the flavors dancing on our tongues. I could never decide which was better, hot or cold schnitzel. He broke the silence after a few minutes.

"When we got back, I checked the bistro to see if there was anything the killer might have dropped. Maybe something small, so I looked in every corner. Nothing. So there goes that theory." He sounded dejected.

"Thank you for everything." I was drifting off again, the half-hour awake having sapped my strength.

CHAPTER EIGHTEEN

As she had not yet seen the finished product, I gave Chloé the tour of the bistro, pouring a nice glass of Marilyn Merlot for her to enjoy. Chloé is a huge Marilyn Monroe fan and squealed when she saw the name of the wine. "Ommagod, I love it! All the funny names, this is so cool!" She lingered in the bar area, glancing at the names of the bottles and admiring the display case.

"Okay, I'll show you the upstairs. My parents are here and it turns out that they'll be moving close by next month."

As we made our way back to the kitchen, I could hear Nicole talking with my mum, who, to my horror, had come down to help. Chloé gave her a big hug, having met her a number of times before when she had briefly been my roommate.

"Mrs. Kis, you're moving here; that's great! It's so good to see you."

"Chloee, nass to see you!" my mother responded, elongating the 'e' at the end of Chloé, which was the only way she could pronounce it. We continued upstairs, leaving Nicole to fend for herself. She was spunky; I knew she could take on Mama.

Giving my dad a kiss on each cheek, Chloe made small talk while I gulped two more Tylenols. Niceties done, I gave her a quick tour of the upstairs then we made our way back down to the bistro.

In the short time we were gone, my mom seemed to have commandeered the kitchen, while Nicole, the traitor, smiled sweetly. I rather suspected she looked relieved, even. I raised a brow.

"Your mum has things under control here, so you sit down and I'll show Chloé the menu and how to work the cash register and how we run things around here. Nora will also be here soon, so I'll give her a refresher, and then I'll oversee things, help where needed once we open, play the piano and sing when I know everything's running smoothly. You, however, are ordered to go back upstairs to relax once its opening time," Nicole instructed as I fought back panic.

Could the place really run without me? Could I trust my mother in the kitchen? What if she clogged everyone's arteries by cooking everything in pig fat, or worse yet, gave everyone fried chunks of pig fat to eat (a Hungarian specialty) and my entire clientele perished in the blink of an eye? I dashed to the kitchen to see what was on the menu.

Mum was singing to herself in Hungarian as she coated the chicken pieces with her special blend—the same one used for the schnitzels—and I could not help but smile. Oh, yes! She was going to make her fried chicken. I suppose I could allow that. Saliva began to pool in my mouth as I anticipated my supper. I knew how to make it but have never divulged the "secret" recipe. Of course, mine never turned out quite like my mother's.

I licked my lips again in anticipation then went back into the bistro area where Nicole was instructing Chloé on how to use the cash register. Clearly everything was under control and I wasn't needed there. I gathered the basket that Nicole had prepared and asked Chloé to drive me down the street to the pizza place since I wasn't allowed to drive yet.

"Come inside with me, will you?" I asked Chloé as I cowered in the car. I wondered how much Leonardo hated me, and why. More importantly, who else did he hate, and had he killed them?

We walked into the restaurant and were greeted by a stumpy man with thick dark hair and a gray moustache. He smiled broadly. "Hello, Madame," he oozed. I froze. It was the man who I'd seen with Harriet downtown.

"I'd like to speak to Mr. Leonardo, please," I said, giving my brightest smile and trying not to sound nervous.

"Thatsa me," he replied. I introduced myself and his smile faded. "Get outta now," he bellowed. "You notta welcome here, you no getta my pizza!"

I talked fast. "Sir, please, take this basket. This is what I serve at the bistro. I don't sell pizza or anything that you have on your menu. I'm not here to compete with you, and I'm not even open every day. I don't know what I may have done to displease you, and I'd like very much for us to be friends."

"No! Out!" he yelled, pointing at the door.

I left the basket on his counter and scurried out quickly, recoiling from his anger and nervous as he started to approach me.

Chloé looked at me with huge eyes. "Why does he hate you so much?"

"I wish I knew. Let's go home, please." It was sobering to know that I wasn't as well liked as I imagined myself to be, especially by someone who wasn't even giving me a chance.

Exhausted from the verbal sparring, I went up to my room for a nap. The sound of faint voices was the next thing I remember. I must have dozed off because it was now dark outside my window. I lay still, trying to determine the source. Ah, I smiled, I knew that sound.

I slowly got up, no dizziness now, and made my way into the dining room. Matt and my dad sat at a table eating fried chicken with homemade potato salad.

Matt leaped up and wrapped me in his arms. I purred. Then I remembered that my dad was there and I pulled away quickly. Sitting down, I piled three pieces of chicken onto my plate with a small spoonful of potatoes. I have never pretended to be a vegetarian, or even entertained the thought.

We ate amidst small talk and I filled Matt in on the news about my parents finding a house, then I inquired if the bistro was still standing in my brief absence.

"Your mum and your friends have everything under control," Matt informed me. "There were a few tables occupied already when I came upstairs, and Nicole was just taking the stage. I know you're curious about how they're handling things. What do you say we go down later and sit in a cozy corner and pretend we're just regular customers?" he suggested. A smile tugged at my lips at the thought.

"Sounds like a great idea!" Yes, perfect. We could actually be on a date and out from under my parents' eyes. And I could keep an eye on things in the bistro.

Once finished, my dad shooed us out of the way, telling us he'd wash the dishes once we'd helped clear the table. I freshened up quickly, slipped into a pair of light blue jeans with a flowy-and showy-pink top and a pair of sexy heels. On a whim, I put on a long reddish-brown wig that I had used the previous Halloween, the hair hanging almost to my bum. It was probably best that I wasn't recognized as Matt and I were still trying to keep the relationship under wraps.

Matt was petting Hummer, who had made himself comfortable on his lap, warming up to him. I would be purring too if I were sitting there, I thought wistfully. As I emerged, Matt's hand froze in mid-stroke. I smiled demurely and held out my hand. "Ready to go—or do you prefer to stay here with Hummer?"

He gave Hum a final scratch behind an ear then gently eased him off. That alone made me like him even more. Showing that he could be kind and considerate with my cat went a long way.

As we were alone, he swiftly crossed the room and put his hands around my waist. There was no smile on his face as he stood there gazing at me. It was more of a searching look. Searching for what, I wasn't sure. He leaned forward, gently grazing my lips with his own. "Did we really only meet less than two weeks ago?" he asked. I had wondered the same thing. Officially, yes, it had only been two weeks.

My knees turned to Jell-O as his tongue tangled with mine. The touch was electric and I couldn't help but let out a contented moan. His response was to back me up against the wall and lean his entire body against mine, his hands on my shoulders, pinning me into position. It had been forever since I'd experienced anything like this, the passion gone from my prior relationship years before it actually ended.

The kiss was long, and by the time it ended our bodies were pressed firmly against each other, leaving little to the imagination. To my surprise, I realized I had one hand cupped around his butt and the other on his chest, inside his shirt, having somehow undone his top two buttons. I looked at him in surprise, unsure how my hands had ended up there. Clearly they had a mind of their own and were not to be trusted. I blushed furiously as I realized where his hands were, both under my top.

"Mmmm, belly button ring," he murmured. "I like. Now, would you care to go on our date before your dad catches us and I'm banned from this house?" We grinned at each other as we reluctantly pried our bodies apart.

We descended to the bistro, entering from the front to make it look like we were customers. Nicole had saved us the most romantic spot, a comfy couch in a corner near the piano area. Matt had gone down to make the request, without me knowing, while I had been getting ready. I shot her a panicked glance.

"Don't worry, everything's going fine, and why are you incognito?!"

"I don't want to be recognized tonight. I think I'll just take a quick peek inside the kitchen". I grabbed her hand and dragged her to the kitchen. I stopped in horror when I saw what my mom was wearing. Yellow sweatpants with one of my bistro tops proclaiming, "Do you think I'm *Sexy?*" in red and black. Sexy being one of the wines we carry, of course.

"She doesn't go out to see the customers, right?" I hissed at Nicole. She shook her head. "No, she's stayed in here the entire time. She's almost done frying the chicken, which she'll leave in the oven, and then she's heading back upstairs."

"Okay, make sure no one sees her, and I mean *no one*!" I grimaced again, not sure which was worse, that top or the yellow pants.

I approached my mom, and shaking off the grimace I gave her a big kiss on the cheek and thanked her for her help and asked if she was having fun. She admitted it was very tiring but that she was happy to help and that Nora and Chloé had passed on many compliments about the chicken. She looked proud about the compliments and I felt a stab of appreciation. At the mention of her name, Nora popped in. She scrutinized me.

"How's your noggin, Mali?" she asked with concern.

"Much better, Nora, and thank you so much for your help tonight."

"Hey, I don't mind. It gets me away from the man for a few hours. He's driving me crazy these days." Like all couples who've been together a very long time, Nora cherished an occasional time away from her *better half*.

"And speaking of men, is that the juicy morsel from New Years that you're with?"

I grinned, blushing. "Yes, that's him. But..." my voice

trailed. Both Nora and Nicole waited, with raised brows..."I think I'm falling for him way faster than I wanted to, and it's scaring me a little," I finally admitted.

"Well, how long have you been seeing him?" Nora asked.

"Less than two weeks."

"Oh, boy, you got it bad. Can't blame you though, he sure looks tasty."

Nicole squeezed my arm, smiling briefly. "Just enjoy it and have fun; don't overthink things," she said then added a bit bitterly, "while it lasts, anyway." She disappeared, leaving me pondering. Why the bitterness? Trouble with Sean, perhaps?

I joined Matt on the couch and he snuggled closer, wrapping an arm around my shoulders and pulling me flush against his side. My skin tingled with excitement.

Listening to Nicole's advice and not wanting to over analyze, I pushed my fears aside and sank back against the cushions. Nicole brought me a coffee and brought Matt a glass of wine then took the stage.

While she crooned one of my favorites, Diana Krall's "The Look of Love", Matt pulled me even closer.

Nicole sang a few more songs while Chloé and Nora served the customers. At some point, Nora swung by to give Matt a refill, winking at me and leaning forward to whisper the name of the wine in my ear while she flashed the bottle at me. "Holy Cow." That meant she was impressed, just in case I'd missed her undressing him with her eyes. Nora was feisty, and I had to suppress a laugh. It was not lost on Matt, who blushed under her scrutiny.

"What did she whisper to you?" he asked after she'd moved on.

"We do this thing where we try to match the name of the wine with a situation or our impression of someone or the scenario." I grinned. "You're drinking a Chardonnay called, Holy Cow."

His lips twitched in an embarrassed smile. "I usually

have red, but this is quite nice. Does that mean she approves?"

"Oh yes!" I replied. Then added flirtatiously, "Nora has a good eye."

"Are these three ladies your closest friends?"

"Yes, hands down. I've known Nicole since I was twelve. We bonded on the first day of grade seven. I met both Nora and Chloé at my previous job, and we became close friends. I don't have many friends, but the ones that I do have are keep-for-life, and I wouldn't have it any other way."

He looked wistful, and that look reminded me of his earlier frown. "Hey, earlier, when you mentioned that you'd called Sean for Nicole's number, you frowned and looked...I don't know....confused. What was that about?"

His eyes moved to the stage where Nicole was just finishing a song. He frowned slightly again. He started to speak then paused, shaking his head.

"It's probably nothing. For some reason, I thought Sean was married, but I could be wrong. I don't know him on a personal level, just professionally."

Interesting... This, combined with Nicole's sudden flash of bitterness? There might be a connection. I vowed to find out later, but in the meantime I relaxed and leaned my head on Matt's shoulder, breathing in his cologne. He shifted slightly and I felt his fingers on my neck, rubbing gently. Oh, hello... My neck bones were connected to my loin bones, and a jolt of electricity zagged right down between the two. With the sudden rush of blood, I felt my cheeks flaming. He must have felt the heat too.

"Are you feeling feverish? Maybe I should take you back upstairs to lie down. I forgot that you're supposed to be taking things easy today. Maybe I was rushing things by suggesting that we come down here?" The worry in his eyes only warmed me further.

Pulling myself together, I figured I should cool the mood down and tell him about Leonardo. "I was just remembering my earlier run-in with the owner of the pizza place. Matt, he hates me, yet I've never met him or done anything to him!"

He nodded. "That doesn't surprise me. Leo can be pretty hot-blooded. He liked having the only place in town where you could grab a bite to eat. You might not serve the same stuff, but you're still a threat. I think he's all bark and no bite, but it's probably best to stay clear of him just in case. I don't think he got along with the former owners of this place either." Great! Just what I'd wanted to hear. But how in the world did Matt know all this?

He broke off as we were interrupted by the vibrating of his cell phone in his blazer pocket. He apologized and looked at the number, apologized again and answered. His side of the conversation was full of 'yes's' and 'uh-huh's'. A 'this wasn't the best time, but he'd be there shortly'. A sigh and another 'yes'. I thought I heard a woman's voice, but I couldn't be certain.

He took my hand and stood, lifting me with him then wrapped both arms around me for a short hug. "I'm sorry, but I have to take care of something that can't wait, but we'll pick up where we left off another night."

"Uh, yeah, sure..." I replied, trying to hide my disappointment. The Charlie Brown voice on the other end of his phone bothered me. The more I thought about it, the more I was sure it was a woman.

He asked if he could bring me back upstairs but I declined, saying I'd stay to finish my coffee. This time when he kissed me, it was brief.

I curled up on the couch with my coffee and snacked on tortilla chips dipped in garlic hummus. Nicole had finished singing and was now serving customers. I was trying to catch her eye to get her to join me when something else caught my eye.

A chill ran up my spine.

CHAPTER NINETEEN

At first my eyes had just skimmed past the two guys sitting at a table. Then that gypsy feeling tingled my nerves.

It wasn't unusual to have two girls sitting together in the bistro, or a mixed group, or a couple. Two guys, however, wasn't common, unless it was Men's Monday, which it wasn't, and that may have been what my subconscious first picked up. I studied them for a moment; both wore heavy beards, like something out of *Duck Dynasty*. I don't mean to stereotype, but this wasn't my usual clientele. And what further caught my eye was how both men were dressed in business suits. The look struck me as a costume.

It didn't take long to notice that they were especially interested in my friends as they went about serving. In fact, their eyes were practically glued to them, however they did not notice me, apparently a single female all by myself on a couch with flowing red hair and showing a bit of cleavage in my pink top. For a good ten minutes, I studied them as they studied my friends, trying to understand what my damaged brain was trying to tell me.

Before I could make the connection, they stood to

leave and waited by the cash register to pay their bill. Just as one of the Grizzly's' was leaving, I caught a different view of his profile. Perhaps it was the way the light glinted at just the right angle, or perhaps it was the expression on his face, but just as he dashed out the door, my eyes widened as my brain screamed the answer at me.

It may have been the man who had followed Nicole and me when we were downtown. We hadn't gotten a great look at him that day, of course. I could have been wrong, but I didn't think so. Obviously in disguise, he was here for a reason, and that couldn't be good. Were these two the ones who were here on New Year's Eve with the man who was killed?

I called Matt with trembling fingers, but the call went straight to voicemail. I left a message: *the man who followed me was here tonight.* A moment later, I shot to my feet. Maybe they were still in the parking lot.

I made it to the door before the black and white dots in my head disabled me. I stood looking out, but not seeing anything beyond the dots as I swayed. I had gotten up far too quickly and the headache was returning. My eyes scanned the lot. No sign of movement. I couldn't help thinking that Matt was also gone, and I couldn't even reach him. Some of the doubt returned but I quickly brushed it aside. I had to learn to trust him.

I grabbed Nicole's arm and dragged her to the couch. "The guy who was following us downtown was here!" I explained excitedly. "I tried to call Matt but got his voicemail. Do you think you should call Sean?" Her eyes clouded for a moment and I instantly felt bad. I seemed to have struck a nerve. "Are you still seeing Sean?" I asked gently.

She puffed out her lips in a long sigh. "Well, I think so. Other than the night he came here with his buddies, I usually see him pretty early for breakfast, because he often works nights and that's about the time he finishes, but I haven't seen him the past few days, and he hasn't called." I was surprised. Nicole doesn't like mornings, so if she was willing to get up early for a breakfast date, then that was a sure sign that she was serious.

"Maybe he's just been stuck on a case. Or he's out of town," I suggested.

"I suppose. He did say that that can happen. But I figured he'd at least text or something."

"Well, if he's working nights, he should be on duty now, right?"

"True," she agreed. "Let me try to call."

She returned a few minutes later, a frown creasing her forehead. "I only got his voicemail at his work number, so I tried his cell." Her frown deepened. "I got an answer to the text I sent almost right away and it said "who is this?" She looked up at me, her eyes glassy. "What do you think is going on?"

I thought about all the puzzle pieces and another piece fell into place. When Matt had mentioned that he'd called Sean for Nicole's number, it had been during the day. Since they only knew each other professionally, he would have called him at work, meaning he was working a day shift, not a night shift. Not to mention he'd been here on Monday night, and not on duty. Something felt awfully wrong about all this. Instead of voicing my concerns, I pasted a smile on my face and suggested an alternative. "Maybe something happened to his phone and he lost all his contact numbers. And, by the way, how'd your date go the other night with that other guy?" Maybe some distraction would help lighten her spirits.

Her face screwed up slightly. "He got weirder by the minute. He kept insisting that I let him drive me home, but I always make sure I have my own car. I could have sworn he was following me, so I drove down some wrong streets for a while until I was sure I'd lost him. Anyway, about Sean... I guess that could make sense. But that doesn't mean he couldn't have called me here or stopped by. And he knows where I work during the day, too. You know what? I'm not going to answer that text. If it's him, he knows where to find me. In the meantime, I've got work to do." With that, she squared her shoulders and stood, returning for last call orders.

Exhausted from all the adrenaline, I heaved myself upstairs. My parents were already in bed so I triple-checked all locks then gratefully climbed into my bed after a snack of two Tylenols.

HUNGARIAN GOULASH

Is it a soup? Is it a stew? You decide. Don't be daunted by the ingredients- you choose only the veggies you want.

    1 pound cubed stewing beef, cubed small
    1 onion chopped
    1 diced tomato
    1 green and 1 red pepper (small) diced
    2 large cubed uncooked potatoes
    4 cloves of garlic, chopped
    2 large carrots, chopped
    2 celery stalks, chopped
    Mushrooms- whole or sliced, doesn't matter
    1/4 cup sour cream (light, regular, doesn't matter)
    1 small turnip or parsnip, diced
    Spices & Herbs: 1 tablespoon each: Paprika, garlic powder, parsley, dill
    1 teaspoon or so of salt and a few shakes of pepper
    1 teaspoon mustard and 1 tablespoon ketchup

You can either choose whatever veggies you have at home, what you like, or all of the above. That's what makes this recipe so versatile. This is how I make it and not necessarily the real Hungarian way since the real Goulash doesn't usually have this many vegetables. For example, my parents never ever bought or cooked celery. If you want to make it even healthier, you can also add a can of chickpeas or white kidney beans or a handful of lentils of some sort.

In about 3 tablespoons of whatever oil you like to use, brown the cubed beef over medium heat. Once browned, add chopped onions and garlic. Stir for a few minutes. Next, add all of your spices and stir until blended and then add water just until the meat is covered. Next, add all of the remaining ingredients. Turn heat a bit lower so that it's simmering slightly rather than a raging boil. Stir every 10 minutes or so. Should cook to nice and tender within about 30 to 40 minutes. You may have to add a bit more water, but usually it's good. Taste test to see if it needs any more salt or anything else.

Serve with: Traditionally, egg noodles or other homemade noodle type things that's too complicated to get into here. Keep it simple: cook up store bought egg noodles. Or even easier, serve over top of rice. I've even served it over mashed potatoes or regular pasta like rotini.

The above can also be made with diced chicken, veal or pork instead of beef.

CHAPTER TWENTY

My parents went back to Montreal the next morning, apparently satisfied after peering outside and seeing that there had been surveillance during the night and assuming I would be safe. I did not tell them about the Beards and how no one had been around protecting me at that time. Why worry them? And really, I desperately wanted my space back.

The weekend came and went. My only contact with Matt had been a text saying, "Got your message and I beefed up security. Back on Wednesday. Stay out of trouble."

I bristled.

Adding fuel to my inner fire, I googled how much surveillance would cost and was staggered by my findings. I hoped that Matt wasn't running me a tab at several thousand dollars a week and wondered again what his motive was for offering help without charge. Was it merely to help find his friend's killer? How long was he willing to foot the bill? Perhaps he thought I'd repay the debt with sexual favors? And if faced with that proposition, would I?

Nicole fared no better, without a single text or visit

from Sean. Her mood fluctuated between flippant, then bitter, then sad, and then determined to forget him. She even had a date lined up for Tuesday night with someone new. I envied her and wondered why Matt had had to leave so suddenly, who The Voice was, and why was he away for so long? Did he have a wife tucked away? But no, Joey's girlfriend gave no indication of anything like that. Kids maybe? He'd never mentioned any, but that didn't mean anything, of course.

By Monday I was no longer having headaches and was in full swing with the last minute planning for the Murder Mystery dinner taking place in two days. The person in charge of the production met me in the bistro and had brought long tables for the event.

The piano area was sectioned off by screens, and we stored as much of my furniture as we could in that section, where the actors would go once they were "killed off". What didn't fit was trucked away into storage for a couple of days. We went over the menu and timing of each course as all the details had to be in perfect sync with the act that would be played out. I was interrupted by my cell phone ringing.

"Yeah, I had a message about New Year's Eve..." I stiffened, thinking quickly and remembering the day I had been calling people who had been here that night, trying to find out information.

"Yes, sir, thank you for calling. Did you know the gentleman who was found in my bistro?"

"How'd you get my number?" he barked.

"It was in our reservation book."

"Oh. Okay. No, actually, I didn't know the guy, but I was calling because I lost my lighter and wondered if it's there. It had sentimental value, so I was wondering if you've found one."

My arm hair was standing on end. This conversation was bizarre. Before I could stop myself, I blurted, "What a coincidence, we actually did. What color is it?"

Clearly he wasn't expecting that. "You know, I'm not sure I ever really noticed. Green, I think. I actually never use it, but it was in my coat pocket."

"I see. The one I found was blue." I was fishing.

"Yeah, mine could be blue, now that I think about it," he replied. For some reason, he wanted whatever lighter I supposedly might have.

"Well, I'm so glad you called then. Can you come pick it up on Wednesday night, say around eight," I suggested. That was when the murder mystery dinner would be ending, so there would be people milling about. This guy was clearly nervous about something.

He agreed, and as he hung up, I heard odd laughter in the background. My hackles rose. I'd heard that laugh before, but where?

I spent most of Tuesday running errands for supplies I needed and prepping whatever I could in advance. I'd be lying if I said I didn't check my cell every half hour or so, only to be faced with disappointment each time. Matt had said he'd be back Wednesday, but I'd be busy that day, so I likely wouldn't see him until Thursday, almost a full week since the last time I'd seen him.

My last stop was the corner grocery store for a blue lighter. As I paid, the old lady at the cash tsk-tsk'd me. I glanced up, surprised and confused. "A pretty girl like you shouldn't be smoking. It's not good for you."

I smiled kindly. "Oh, I don't smoke, ma'am. I use it to light candles. I'm the owner of the Whine and Cheese bistro just down the street. My name is Amalia." I held out my hand, intending to shake hers, when she recoiled. I looked down to see if my hand had offensive particles on it.

"You can't be in here. Mr. Leonardo will be very unhappy. He gives us a lot of business, you see, so we really can't have you here. Please, please go." She practically threw the lighter at me and shooed me out the door before I could say another word.

What was it with Leonardo? He was starting to piss me off. I pocketed the lighter then walked down to the other end of the building to the pizza place. I must have been visibly fuming because those around me gave me a curious look and then scuttled out of my path. Intending to give him a piece of my mind, I stormed in with all the power of a tsunami. Spotting my prey, I no sooner opened my mouth to speak when a big bat of pepperoni whizzed past my ear.

"Out!" he roared. My courage vanished as quickly as it had appeared and I darted outside to the sanctity of my car. I drove the short distance back to the bistro, suddenly smirking because I had managed to snag the pepperoni 'weapon' on my way out. Victory, albeit a small one, was mine.

Intending to turn into my parking lot, I realized that the adrenaline was still coursing through my body and I found myself sailing past my house on a new mission. I had time to kill, so why not poke around and put the energy to good use? I continued down the road a few minutes, and then stopped in front of the gate that blocked Joey's house. I parked on the road and stared at the house, mustering my nerve. I had thought of stopping by a number of times to offer my condolences to Eunice, Joey's girlfriend, especially since I had almost been the one to tell her the news of his death during our first meeting. Making up my mind once and for all, I took a deep breath and marched up to the door.

I paused before knocking, suddenly doubting myself again. Maybe I should just leave her alone, I reasoned. After all, it was unlikely I'd ever see her again anyway. But then again, if I was being honest, I wasn't totally satisfied that she hadn't had something to do with his murder. After all, the police always suspect those who were the closest to the victim. I wondered if she was still on their suspect list, or if they even cared about it anymore.

I leaned over to the window next to the door and

peeked inside, shielding the glare from the sun off the window pane by cupping my hands on either side of my eyes. Through the sheer curtains on the other side of the pane, I could make out Eunice in jeans and a t-shirt, tossing items into boxes that were still scattered about. The scene was much the same as the last time I'd been here, except this time, the place seemed a lot emptier and dozens of boxes were stacked in neat piles.

Satisfied that she was home, I was again about to knock when something odd caught my ears—just a faint sound, but a familiar one. I pressed my ear against the window, feeling only a touch of guilt.

"'Tis the season to be jolly," she sang with apparent glee, then belted out, "Fa la la la lala la la la," loud and clear, tossing a number of items haphazardly into a box and then reaching for a glass on the table from which she belted back a shot of something. She then tilted her head back and laughed to herself.

I stepped away from the window quickly before she glanced my way. I had very little experience in dealing with grief, since no one close to me had ever passed away, but I had heard that people can react bizarrely. I was left feeling both intrigued and unsettled.

I pounded on the door and waited, mentally rehearsing my greeting. The door opened a crack and Eunice peered out, her eyes round like saucers. "May I help you?" she asked very quietly, in stark contrast with how she'd been bellowing out the tunes just moments earlier.

"Hello, Eunice. We met not long ago. I'm Amalia." She stared at me blankly. "Matt's girlfriend," I elaborated. She still stared at me blankly. "I popped by a while ago and dropped off his hat that he'd forgotten at my home. I just wanted to extend my condolences about Joey."

"Oh, thank you." she said flatly, then relapsed into silence.

"Can I help you in any way? Maybe get you something, or give you hand packing? Anything?" I rambled, unnerved by her lack of hospitality.

"Thank you," she said again, rather stiffly. "I'm good. The packing is almost done. Joey would be happy that these things are finally boxed up. It's just a shame that he isn't here to see it."

"That's right, I remember that you told me that the two of you were starting to pack things together and that he had been getting counselling to help overcome the hoarding. That was incredibly strong of you to stand by him and support him like that," I said kindly, thinking that perhaps I was finally getting past her emotionless exterior.

"Well, when the heart is set on something..." She let the sentence trail off then nodded at me. "Thank you for coming, but I must return to my task." She gestured at the boxes behind her. "I have to get all this settled soon." She gave me a tight smile, but before I could think of anything else to say, she closed the door. I was dismissed.

The visit left me perplexed. I would have to discuss it with Matt once he was back. He knew her better, so maybe he could help me make sense of it.

I returned home and puttered about cleaning things that didn't need cleaning. It is how I deal with stress.

After cleaning everything I could think of to clean it was four in the afternoon and I still had time to kill. Prowling about like a restless cat, my eyes landed on my purse, so I dumped the contents for a thorough organizing. I'm always downsizing, hoping that the smaller I go, the less junk I will collect. I was down to the size of a mini iPad Air at this point and still managed to cram it full of crap.

Discovering the Victoria's Secret gift card I'd gotten at Christmas from naughty Nora, I thought I might shop for something sexy. My practical mind suggested a flannel PJ set, but my hormones suggested something else entirely...

I decided to go through my drawers and take stock of what I had. To my dismay, I discovered that I had no sexy underclothes. Practical underwear, yes; and lots of PJ's, but nothing sexy. A sudden thought struck me. Matt would be back Wednesday. Was I Ms. Wednesday Night after all?

I stormed out the door and went to the mall. Two hours later, I was home with a big bag of colorful, silky, sexy goodies and a belly full of gyros and poutine. Stomach protruding from the feast, I decided it wasn't a good time to model my purchases for Hummer. He'd have to take my word for it. The look he gave me suggested he didn't care either way.

Seven-thirty. Still early. I settled down on the couch but was too nervous to relax. I called Nicole but then was about to hang up, remembering she had a date, when, to my surprise, she answered.

"Hi, Nicole. I almost hung up because I didn't think you'd still be home. I actually forgot you have a date tonight," I apologized, ready to hang up.

"Actually, I cancelled," she admitted. "I was pretty freaked out over that last date being so creepy. Clearly, I'm not having any luck these days. I hate to admit it, but I also realized that I really do like Sean, so maybe I'll give him the benefit of the doubt. I'll wait a bit longer to see if I hear from him again before I move on. I'm glad you called though, because I'm feeling pretty restless. You wouldn't feel up to doing something, would you?"

We agreed to meet at a pub halfway between our homes at nine-thirty. I peered out cautiously before leaving and noted that the surveillance was back in place for the night. Before going to my car, I walked over to the man on guard. Maybe it would be Ricky, and I could pump him for information about Matt. I was almost at the car when I slipped on an icy patch and flailed my arms to regain my balance.

It wasn't Ricky, but oh my, he wasn't hard on the eyes. Flustered by his good looks and embarrassed by my windmill impression, I thanked him for keeping watch over me and tried to sound nonchalant as I asked if he'd heard from Matt recently.

"No ma'am, but I'm the night crew. Matt doesn't usually work nights."

"What are your orders?" I wondered.

"Keep you safe, ma'am, and make sure no one who looks suspicious gets close to you, and to follow anyone who does."

"Okay, then you'll want to know that I'm going to a pub and some guy who's been following me was here the other night, so you might want to come with me. May as well have some fun, right? And that way, if I'm followed there, I can point him out to you and you can do whatever it is that you do."

I had to admit, even though I was trying to be casual, I was still spooked by the visit of the two strange looking men the other night and the way they'd been watching my staff. Not to mention the crazy disguise and that I was pretty sure they were the same men from New Year's Eve.

I had another motive too, of course. He was damn hot and I thought he might take Nicole's mind off things. I sent her a text to give her a heads-up regarding my company, and she was already there when we walked in. She was looking pretty glum but her eyes lit up when she caught sight of my companion, and I could see her smooth her hair quickly as we approached. Hair, I may add, that already looked impeccable and nicely styled, unlike my own scruffy ponytail.

About to introduce them, I realized I'd neglected my manners and hadn't asked him his name. "I'd like to introduce my friend Nicole, but I'm sorry, I don't even know your name yet," I apologized.

"Sean," he replied with a smile, taking Nicole's hand in his. Really, Sean? Another one? Nicole's smile slipped slightly at the mention of the name. "Did I say something wrong?" he asked, catching the subtle change in mood.

"No, sorry, it's just....I was seeing someone named Sean and then I just stopped hearing from him, so...." her voice faded. No further explanation required. The implication that she might have been jilted was clear.

New Sean shook his head. "Well, he's crazy, and it's his loss." He slid into the booth next to Nicole and her eyes caught mine. I could read the message loud and clear. It said, "Thank you, this is just what I needed!"

"Excuse me while I use the ladies room. Can you please order me a diet Black Raspberry if the waitress comes by?" Being a very good friend, I figured I'd give them a few minutes to chat without me hanging around. I took my time in the ladies room and by the time I returned to the table, they were chattering away and my drink was waiting for me.

I'd only been sitting a few minutes when the hackles on my neck rose. Okay, I don't really have hair on my neck, despite being European, but it's the same feeling. From where I was sitting, I could see everyone entering the pub. I thought my eyes were playing tricks on me. It was getting late, after all, and my contact lenses were getting cloudy. I blinked a few times and gave them a quick rub then re-focused on my prey.

Old Sean had just walked into the pub. He certainly didn't look like he was dressed for duty on the night shift since he was wearing jeans and a hoodie. The lady with him wasn't dressed like a cop either. And the hand on his arm had a ring big enough for me to see from across the room. To my relief, they sat at the opposite end of the pub in a section not visible from where we were sitting.

I downed my drink, shooter style, and told New Sean that my head was hurting and that I needed a bit of air. Would he mind coming with me just to make sure the parking lot was safe?

Before Nicole could join us, I asked her to order me a coffee whenever she could snag the waitress, and then I rushed off without waiting for an answer, noting the confused look on her face. Sean shrugged and followed me, stopped me at the door and went out first, nodding to me after taking stock of the surroundings.

Once outside, I talked fast. "Sean, I'm really sorry to drag you into this, especially when you don't even know us, but the Sean that Nicole had been seeing just walked in with another woman, and I think he's married. She'll be so humiliated if she sees them so we have to get her out of there somehow, and fast."

He nodded. "Leave it to me," he replied.

We waited a moment so that Nicole didn't wonder why we'd been so quick when I claimed to need some air. Squinting, I could see someone sitting in a car, having a smoke. This isn't unusual, really. In Ottawa, there's a by-law that you can't smoke inside public places, and since it was cold outside, the person likely had decided to smoke in the car. What was unusual, though, was that no one had come out after us, and no new cars had arrived.

I was pondering this and debated if I should mention it when Sean nudged me back inside. We joined Nicole, and moments later the waitress arrived with my coffee. Before she slipped away, Sean asked her for our bill. "What? We just got here!" Nicole exclaimed, looking even more confused than earlier.

"Sorry, Nicole, but your friend here almost blacked out again while we were outside so we have to get her home to rest. I've got my orders to keep her safe and I'm going to drive her home in her car, but I'll need my vehicle afterward. Would you mind following us and then giving me a lift back to my car? I hate to trouble you...."

Oh my, he was smooth. He had found a way to make our story sound credible, make himself sound like a nice guy and to also snag some alone time with her.

"Of course! I'm so sorry, I completely forgot about the concussion. I shouldn't have asked you to come out tonight, Mali. Let's go!"

The waitress arrived with our bill and Sean threw down a bunch of cash despite our protests. Perhaps he had an expense account. I made a mental note to check with Matt, if I ever saw him again.

By a stroke of luck, we made it out the door without seeing Old Sean. Inside my car, New Sean drove, sticking to the story he'd concocted so as not to make Nicole suspicious of our sudden departure. He called his dispatcher, advising him that there was a slight glitch in plans and could someone be sent to watch my house in his place for a couple of hours and that he'd explain later but not to worry, there was no danger.

And it all sounded so plausible.

CHAPTER TWENTY-ONE

*H*e dropped me off and then headed over to Nicole's car with a a smile on his face and a spring to his step. Waving as acknowledgement to the car already idling in my parking lot, they drove off.

I was still fidgety from having seen Nicole's ex, so I went down to the bistro to see if there were any details I could tend to in advance. As I unlocked the door leading from the secret stairway to the office area, I heard something crunch underneath my feet.

I stood listening. The old expression "the silence was deafening" was an understatement. Hearing nothing besides the sound of my own blood pounding in my ears, I edged forward. I peered at the back door, which was firmly closed. I started to head in the direction of the kitchen when the feeling of being cold registered. My eyes flew to the door again and it was then that I noticed that part of the window had been broken.

I turned and flew back up the stairway, remembering to trip the locks. Once upstairs, I went to the front window and flicked the lights on and off several times, then left them on and stood at the window flapping my arms like a chicken. Silly, yes, but I had no clue how to contact the guy in the surveillance car.

The person on duty was slow to react. I kept flapping my arms in a panic and wondered what was taking him so long. Finally, I saw him leave the car and head up the stairs to my living quarters, and relief washed over me. I ran to the door, opened the locks and threw the door open. "Thank God you're here! Someone has broken in downstairs and I don't know if they're still here!" I babbled, practically dragging him to the inner stairway after bolting the door again.

He smiled and his nicotine stained teeth were a stark contrast from New Sean's dazzling whites. I caught a whiff of cigarettes and figured I must have interrupted his smoke, which would explain the long wait for him to get out of the car.

"You stay up here, ma'am, and I'll check it out down there. Don't come down until I knock on this door and say open sesame. Be sure to stay here." He gave me another smile and winked.

Although he did not win any awards for originality, nor for oral hygiene, the rest of him was neat and tidy and he seemed competent enough. He didn't have the bulky build that Sean did, but if Matt had hired him, then he would surely be able to handle the situation.

I closed and locked the door behind him and paced for what seemed like an eternity, his presence lingering by way of the smell of stale cigarettes. A decade later, at the sounds of a knock and the not-so-secret code, I rushed to open the door.

"Everything's in order, ma'am. Sorry I took so long; I found some tape and cardboard and patched up the window for you." He took off the gloves he'd been wearing and crammed them into his pocket. "I looked around, and there's no one down there—probably some kids that were up to no good. You have nothing to worry about, so I'll be going now." With that he rushed out the door.

I made a mental note to replace the back door with one that had no window, even though a cross breeze coming from the back would have been so nice during summer. I watched him through the window, thankful that Matt had arranged for surveillance. At the bottom of the stairs, he stopped to light a cigarette before continuing toward the car, and as I continued to watch, he climbed into the front seat. On the passenger side.

Confused, I leaned closer to the window, my nose pressed flat against it. Seeing me, a hand shot out and waved, and the car shot forward and out onto the street. I was still standing there a minute later, trying to figure out what had just happened, and why he'd left, and who was driving, when another car entered my lot. Seeing me in the window, the man hurried up to the house. I hurried to the door, alarm bells clanging in my head.

"Who are you?" I yelled through the closed door, my cell phone clutched firmly in hand.

"My name's Josh; I'm with the security company. Sorry I'm late ma'am; they sent me as quickly as they could but Sean didn't give us much time. He shouldn't have left until I got here, but I guess he must have had some sort of emergency. Is everything okay, Ms. Kis?"

I was thoroughly confused. "But when I got home, there was already somebody here, which is why Sean left," I yelled back.

"No, Ms. Kis; I'm the only one they've sent to replace him."

Suddenly, my knees started to wobble. I knew he was telling the truth—he'd called both Sean and myself by name, so clearly he was familiar with him. I suddenly realized that I hadn't even asked the other man his name, and that I had, in fact, literally dragged him into my home. Feeling sick, I threw open the door. "Someone else was here. Up here! And downstairs, too! I let him in, thinking it was you, but then I noticed that there was another person with him in the car when he left!"

His features turned pale. "Ma'am, please call 911 now for backup. I'm going downstairs for a look."

I led him to the inside stairs, and for the second time that evening a man went into the bistro for a look around. This was the most male action I'd had in ages!

While he was still searching, the police arrived, yet again none that I recall having seen before. I explained what had happened and mentioned the murders, the rock through my window, being followed, and the two men who were here in the car, so that they had the big picture.

Josh returned to brief one of the police officers, confirming that someone had actually taken the time to tape cardboard over my broken window and that everything seemed in order. They, too, searched inside and out, with nothing to report other than the broken and patched window. It was a very polite break-in, ma'am. There have been lots of break-ins in the area. We're working on it. When they mentioned that they would dust for prints, I told them not to bother because the man was wearing gloves.

Clearly, someone was after something, but with such minimal damage and the alleged suspects already gone, the police left, satisfied after hearing that I already had surveillance and that it didn't appear as though anyone wanted to harm me.

Frustrated, I tried calling Matt again. No answer. Where could he be this time of night?! I texted him. *Another break-in. Where are you Matt?* I didn't know what else to write.

About ten minutes later, I heard the sound of car doors slamming and looked out to see that Sean had returned and was being informed of what had happened. He nodded then headed up to my door as Josh drove away.

"I'm very sorry, and I take full responsibility. I shouldn't have assumed the car that was here was my replacement." He was blushing furiously from his blunder.

"I assumed the same thing, Sean. It's not your fault. There's something I was going to mention earlier but then I got side tracked. When we were in front of the pub, there was someone in a car, smoking. We hadn't seen anyone arrive or go out, which is why I took notice of it when I saw the flash of a lighter. The guy here today lit up as he headed back to the car, so it could have been the same guy. Or one of them..."

He studied me carefully, nodding. "Yes, that would make sense." More nods. "I didn't notice that we were being tailed, but they may have followed us there, stuck around awhile, saw us, then noticed us go back in and figured maybe they had time to come here to look around, except we ended up coming back early."

It was my turn to nod as I remembered something Matt had said. "Matt thinks that whoever is after me either thought I saw or heard something, or possibly they left something here. I wonder if that could be it. The man who came in was polite, was dressed nicely enough, he even patched my window that he broke. But he was down there for quite a while." I blanched when I remembered the phone call about the lighter with "sentimental value". Would someone break in for that now that they thought I had it? Could the lighter somehow connect them to the crimes? Fingerprints, perhaps?

"Let's go," Sean said, taking my elbow and leading me toward the door. We went downstairs and turned on all the lights. "Okay, look around. Is anything missing, even something small that you wouldn't normally notice?"

I inched my way through the place. Nothing seemed to be out of order or missing. The Imposter had even swept up the broken glass for me, which was now in the garbage can. My theory was that he had done this to account for the amount of time he had spent down here. No doubt my arrival home had cut their original search short, and I had provided the perfect opportunity for him to come in and look around at his leisure.

Giving up, we returned upstairs where I made us both a hot chocolate. Again he started to apologize but I interrupted. "Not your fault. But how about telling me where you were for two hours? Your car was parked only fifteen minutes away." I smirked, already suspecting the answer. To my surprise, I was only half right.

CHAPTER TWENTY-TWO

*H*e looked uncomfortable and cleared his throat. "Well, we went back to my car and I was just about to ask her for her phone number but I couldn't quite get up the nerve. You see, I haven't really dated in a while. So we were just doing small talk, you know. She also mentioned that she thought someone had been following her. Not just the two of you, but her alone. And then that guy came out, the one she was dating, with his arm around that woman's waist. Before I could do anything, she shot out of the car and started yelling at him, called him a cheater, then slapped him, and then his woman yelled at him and slapped him, then the two women yelled at each other and started slapping him and each other. It took a while to calm her down and drag her away. I couldn't just leave her on her own like that, so I followed her home. We talked until she had calmed down, and then I came back here as soon as I could."

"So, did you get her phone number?" I asked.

"No," he mumbled.

I smiled and wrote down Nicole's number for him. I was pretty sure she wouldn't mind. Slipping it across the table, I said "You'll want to call her tomorrow to check on her. She'd like that."

He grinned and pocketed the scrap of paper. "Thank you, yes, I'd like to do that. She seemed jittery about someone following her and that's been bothering me too. Maybe I'll give her a hand with that. And maybe it's the same guys who've been after you, though she didn't seem to think so. And now I better get myself outside into that car. I'll be in deep water as it is." His face clouded again as he left the house to return to his post.

What a day! Drained, I crawled into bed, not even caring anymore who broke in, who called or didn't call or where the hell Matt was. Well, okay, maybe I still cared a little. And try as I might, I couldn't help worrying about what Nicole may have gotten herself involved with. Was one of her ex-dates following her?

The next day was as crazy as I knew it would be. We had a full house booked for the Murder Mystery event that was starting at six sharp. We were serving a four course meal, consisting of a cheese plate, soup, the main course with wine, followed by cheese cake and coffee. Although the cast was also responsible for food service, I was on my own for cooking. Nicole would be here by five p.m. to help with plating everything.

She showed up promptly at five, rare for her to be on time, and gave me a big grin. I reached for a bottle of wine that had been on the counter and poured us each a glass as we set about our preparations while the cast held a pre-show meeting in the dining area.

"So, Sean's a nice guy, isn't he?" I asked coyly as I took a sip of the berry and dark cherry flavored wine. My eyes were repeatedly drawn to the label: "The Accomplice."

"Hmpft," she snorted. "Which one?"

"New Sean, of course!" I replied, and then continued, "I know what happened. There was another break-in here last night and when Sean showed up, he filled me in about what happened to you last night. I have to say, he seemed pretty enchanted with you."

She brightened again. "Yeah, he was really sweet, actually. Just before you-know-who came outside with his newest conquest, Sean was telling me how he hasn't dated in a while and made a point of saying he's never been married or had kids. I found that a bit weird, you know, getting so personal in the car, but then got to thinking about things last night. You already knew about the other Sean, didn't you, that he was with someone else? Hey wait...what do you mean there was another break-in?"

I filled her in about what had happened and assured her that all was under control, then returned the conversation to Old Sean.

"Yes, I had suspected," I admitted. "I didn't know for sure, but little things weren't adding up, and then I saw him walk into the pub with her, which is why we had to get you out of there. I didn't want you to see that. But, apparently, you saw it anyway."

"Would you have told me what you knew?" she asked softly.

"Absolutely. I was going to tell you today, after our dinner show. I would never keep anything like that from you, but the timing wasn't right."

She smiled and hugged me. "Well, this new Sean seems like a sweetheart, and he is damn good looking. He called me earlier today to check on me and we were talking forever before he finally worked up the nerve to ask me out." She giggled. "I was about to ask him since I was starting to think he'd chicken out."

I shook my head at her ability to bounce back so quickly. If things fizzled out with Matt, I knew I'd return to my solitary life rather than open myself to the potential for more hurt so quickly.

It was almost opening time. Nicole went into the bistro to light the candles for show time but quickly returned. "Where's that lighter?" she asked.

"The lighters are always in the drawer," I replied,

opening one of the kitchen drawers and pulling out a long BBQ lighter that I would use for the candles. I had already made sure that the so-called sentimental lighter I bought for the exchange later that evening was stored in my purse underneath the counter.

"This will work way better than that small black lighter I've been using lately," she said as she started to walk away.

Alarm bells! I grabbed her arm. "What small black lighter? I only ever buy the long BBQ lighters."

"I've been using one of those small cigarette lighters to light the candles. It was on the office floor one day, flush against the boot tray, and I'd moved it over to the bar area, but it's gone now."

I froze. "When did you find it?" I asked, trying not to sound frantic.

"Maybe a couple weeks ago—I never really thought about it." She turned and walked back into the bistro.

Then the cast director announced it was opening time. I made sure everything was ready then went to unlock the doors. For the majority of the evening, I would be mostly in the kitchen or helping to clear plates. It was now show time, and the lead actor took his spot at the entrance door to greet the arriving guests as the other cast members stood close by, ready to accompany them to their seats. I returned to the kitchen to prepare the bottles of wine with little napkin scarves tied around their necks to catch drips, an old flight attendant trick I had learned a decade earlier during a brief stint in the airline industry.

Twenty minutes later, everyone was seated and the cast set about serving the wine while the lead actor gave the audience some instructions for their part in the murder mystery dinner. Already knowing how the mystery ended after seeing the rehearsal, I had paired the evening with a red and white wine called Mad Housewife.

First the cheese plates were served, with Applewood Smoked Cheddar, a couple of balls of delectable Bocconcini, a slice of Gouda and some Blue Stilton, a nice variety ranging from mild to pungent. I had prepared these in advance and wrapped each plate in plastic wrap that we now quickly removed as we added a handful of fancy crackers to each along with a few grapes.

Nicole and I worked fast to keep up with the servers, and once the main course was served, we had a few minutes to rest and to take a peek into the dining area.

The place was packed. The cast involved the audience in their story and had even planted some cast members as diners who would suddenly end up dead on their plates while sitting next to an actual paying customer.

"Tell me that is not your ex," Nicole whispered to me, pointing in Hans's direction. I groaned in dismay. I hated that he was in the bistro, eating my food and drinking my wine. I squinted to see who he was with and ground my teeth even harder. He was with one of his friends that I'd never liked, and there was no way to tell them to leave without disrupting the show, so I had no choice but to allow them to stay. Anyway, I had no time to sulk about it because our short break was over.

I sent Hans one last glare in the dark then we returned to the kitchen to start brewing coffee and tea and plating the cheesecake. Soon it was time to accept the dirty dishes brought back by the cast members and for the desserts to be whisked away.

The end was near and I wondered if the person coming for the lighter was outside waiting, or if they were the ones that broke in and found the real lighter, if it was indeed their lighter. If they did, that would mean that they were on to me since that lighter was black and I'd told them that I had a blue one. Would they remember a minor detail like that?

It was time for us to bring the bills and collect payment from the customers as, by this time, a number of the cast members had been killed off and our help was needed.

As Nicole handed the bill to one client, she screeched at the top of her lungs as someone appeared behind her and held a knife to her throat.

"Shut up, you man stealer, or I'll cut you open right now," the masked woman growled. Then she shuffled Nicole backward toward the screens, the fake knife digging into her neck as Nicole whimpered as she allowed herself to be dragged away. I chuckled. Having only practiced this scene twice, she had nailed it.

I was collecting the payments as quickly as possible so that I could be off the "set" in time for the grand finale. I hurriedly thanked a customer and quickly counted the cash they had given me to see if they needed change. My eyes widened in surprise at what I found.

CHAPTER TWENTY-THREE

I stared in shock at the bill with black writing on it: Matt's name and phone number. I quickly looked up to see if it was Matt playing a trick on me and my blood froze in my veins as I noticed the long beard. Yes, the beards were back, this time wearing jeans and T-shirts. Beady eyes studied my face and looked down to see what had startled me.

I struggled to regain my composure and smiled. Perhaps it was a grimace. Then recounted the bills, pretending I'd lost my count. It was spot on so I thanked them and casually moved on to the customers next them, not wanting to draw their suspicion, but I could feel their eyes boring into my back.

That is when it hit me: Matt's number had been written on a bill that had been stolen the night of the murder. And the beards had been here not long ago, scoping things out. One of the beards was the same man that had followed Nicole and me downtown—I was now certain of it. The other one might have been the man that had broken into my home last night. I thought I caught a whiff of nicotine. One of these men likely stole that money and

191

murdered the man in the stairwell. But how did Joey fit into all this? And how did the lighter fit in? Had the smoker lost it on the night of the murder? Had they noticed me falter and could they see the clue on the bill, or was it too dark for them to have noticed? Clearly, they hadn't realized that one of the bills had been marked in a way that only I would recognize.

I quickly settled the remaining bills, hurrying so that I could return to the kitchen and call the police. I made time for a quick snarl of disapproval at Hans and his friend then ducked into the kitchen, panic now taking over and making my knees weak. Hands trembling, I realized I had forgotten my cell phone upstairs and I could not access the business phone without being noticed, as it was located in the bar area. I got my spare set of keys to the stairway from my hiding spot under the counter and was just about to set off to get my cell phone when suddenly my head snapped back and I yelped in pain. My head was completely tilted back as a steel grip held my ponytail and was pulling down on it, and pulling me backward as well, off balance, back arched. I screamed, but at the exact same time a piercing shriek emanated from the bistro, drowning out my cry. I managed another scream before a smelly hand clamped down over my mouth. My scream was again drowned out by one from the dining area.

I tried to bite the hand but I was too slow. Before I could do any damage, the hand instead jammed itself deep into my mouth, as far as it would go, making me gag. Bile rose in my throat but before I could react, my captor slammed me forward so that my forehead smashed into the wall. I tried to fight the black dots and kicked backwards, hoping to connect with something, then felt my consciousness fading. The last thing I remembered was a series of shots ringing out in the bistro. I recognized the sounds of the finale and hoped that it was not my own.

I heard the sound of snow crunching underfoot before I felt the cold, and I noticed hands clamped around my ankles and more hands around my wrists. I was being dragged in the snow...and none too gently. I opened my mouth to scream but bile rose in my throat again as my mind cleared and I realized something had been shoved inside my mouth.

With tears streaming out of the corners of my eyes, I desperately fought to hold the vomit back and broke one hand free to claw at my mouth to remove the material that was inside. Luckily, neither my mouth nor my hands were bound, no doubt because my tormentors hadn't had time and hoped that I'd be unconscious long enough for them to do what they intended to do.

"Stop moving or you'll make it worse for yourself," a female voice hissed as she quickly let go of my ankles and threw herself on me, knocking the wind out of my lungs. Unable to breath, I had little time to react and only had one hand free. I aimed for the eyes, hoping to poke them out, but missed my shot. As she grabbed my head and began slamming it onto the ground, I again lost consciousness.

I didn't know how much time had passed. My head was pounding and I had gone blind. Or perhaps it was just dark, I finally decided. I remember wondering what time it was as I tried to stretch my legs. They could only go so far. I felt around with my hands and was met with resistance from all sides, all angles. I listened carefully, concentrating on the sounds I could make out.

In a panic, I clawed around inside my enclosure, realizing that I was in the trunk of a car. I felt a moment of relief. At least it wasn't a coffin.

Knowing we were in motion, I didn't waste my breath screaming but instead tried to find something in the trunk that could be useful. To my despair, there was nothing but me and my desire for self- preservation.

I forced myself to breathe deeply, to be ready for whatever was to happen when we stopped. That would be my only chance. I knew I had to try to use some element of surprise. There were two of them but only one of me. I wriggled around as best as I could, while getting into position, and waited.

I have no estimate as to how long we drove. When we finally stopped, I took some deep breaths, and then listened. One car door slammed—just one—then a faint crunching on the frozen snow, barely audible. Breathe. Then a click—automatic trunk opener. The trunk unlatched and I waited for someone to open it all the way.

I imagined my captor on the other side waiting to see if the trunk would be forced open by me. I didn't move a muscle. I let them think I was still unconscious, or dead.

Suddenly, it lifted and I lashed out with my legs, which I had positioned in that direction. I connected only with an arm, which did no damage but prevented my captor from getting close to me. She cursed and made a grab for my legs, but I flailed them furiously while screaming like a lunatic. I was a Tasmanian devil as I continued to elude her grip, but I knew my energy would not last forever. Hopefully it would outlast hers.

She took a few steps backward, but I kept my legs raised in Venus Flytrap position. I tried to peer around her but could see nothing.

"Hurry up Eunice," her accomplice called from the open window at the front of the car. "Do I have to do this myself?"

"I got it, Fred," she snarled. We stared at each other, she, calculatingly, and I, panting from the recent exertion and my injuries.

"Why?" I managed to croak.

She snorted. "Why couldn't you just stop poking around? And why'd you have to buy that place, anyway?"

"What do you mean," I gasped.

"Snooping around at Joey's... Don't think I didn't realize you just wanted to scope out the property. Probably weren't expecting anyone to be there, were you? And taunting us...calling Fred's house to find out if we were with Jimmy on New Year's Eve. You think I didn't know you were on to me? The only thing I can't figure out is how you pieced things together, and why didn't you just pack up and leave."

I didn't know how I had pieced it together either, since I still didn't have it figured out! Obviously something I'd done along the way had hit the jackpot; now I just had to put it all together, and fast.

"That's right," I bluffed, still panting, "I figured it out, and the police know too. You might get away tonight, but they'll track you down. They've had the place staked out. If I go missing, they'll know exactly where to look, and they have the lighter with the fingerprints."

"Liar! We've already got the lighter," she smirked.

"I switched them," I spat out with false bravado.

Filled with rage, she lunged at me. I didn't react fast enough this time and she was able to grab a leg. I tried to shake free but her grip was strong. She began to pull and I screamed again, flailing blindly with my one free leg, hoping for contact, preferably with her face.

Without warning, the Behemoth let go of me and darted around to the front of the car. The door slammed and the car started all before I could scramble out of the trunk. I could see flashing lights behind us in the distance and I grabbed onto the trunk opening with one hand while waving the other frantically as we gained speed.

Afraid of falling out of the car and hitting the pavement at the speed we were now traveling, I sank back into the trunk.

The car behind us was gaining speed and soon I could see that there appeared to be three. The sound of the siren reached my ears and I heaved a sigh of relief, sensing safety was near. The trunk flapped about in the wind and I kept myself low, hugging the bottom.

The flashing lights came closer, though we must have been going well over a hundred miles per hour on a dark country road. Suddenly, the car fishtailed. The driver slowed slightly but quickly regained control and picked up speed again.

The impact was sudden and unexpected. All my focus had been on the lights behind us, and unable to see what was ahead, I had not expected it and I lurched in my small space. The crunch of metal was deafening as we spun, then the crunch of more metal. Then, the only sound was the wailing siren and my ragged breathing.

CHAPTER TWENTY-FOUR

*T*he police car slid to a stop. "Quick, get the girl," I heard, as two more cars pulled up. I heard my name being shouted as an officer peered inside the trunk and asked if I could move. I nodded mutely and he reached forward, extending his hand.

I grabbed the hand just as Matt's face appeared next to the cop. "Let me do it," he barked, reaching in as well and pushing the officer slightly out of his way. I'm not even sure about the logistics of how they got me out since my body was taut with fear and all that registered was that Matt was back in town.

I heard the words "shock" and "blanket" before I let go and slipped into the blackness.

I'm told that it was sometime the next day when I awoke from what felt like a very deep sleep. I remembered very little from the past twenty hours. A few times I remembered opening my eyes and seeing my mom. Then Matt. Dad. Chloé, Nora and her husband. Snippets of conversation, some in Hungarian, that I didn't have the energy to concentrate on. I wondered briefly where Hummer was and if my brother would visit.

Matt was sitting on a chair next to what I assumed was a hospital bed. I had no doubt that I had another concussion and was starting to envision another episode of being fed bacon in bed when he glanced up from the book he was reading. He shot forward in his chair, grabbing my hand.

"Hey Bruiser! How you feeling?" He lifted my hand to his lips, kissing it gently.

"You should see the other guys," I slurred, my tongue sticking inside my dry mouth.

"I did see the other guys. I may even have given one of them a black eye on your behalf," he said, his mouth turning into a thin line.

"So I guess they both lived? What exactly happened in the car?"

"The driver thought he was superman, but the car that had the right of way didn't agree and t-boned into the passenger side, flipping the car around. A light post stopped the spin, again on the passenger side. He was lucky his side wasn't hit. Joey's girlfriend, Eunice, wasn't so lucky. Oh, but we managed to save this," he said as he put my deposit bag on the bed next to me.

"The bistro's money?" I was confused. "How does the money figure into all this? And Joey? And the other man?"

"It was all about money and land. Poor Joey actually didn't have too much to do with this other than falling in love with someone who was using him to try to get his land." I remembered Eunice's words about what the heart wants. I guess she meant his land and not him.

"Enough about this for now though. I've been told that you're not to talk too much and that you have to get lots of rest." He grinned and brushed my bangs out of my eyes. Again, not the way my mother does. Then I remembered that I was mad at him.

"There's something I need to know. I don't play games, so I'm not going to be coy. Quite frankly, I just don't have the energy for that. The last time I was with you, you got a call, then you split with no warning and I didn't see you again until I was almost dead. Who's the woman that called you and why haven't I heard from you?" The ball was now in his court.

Hearing my simple summary of recent events seemed to surprise him. His brows rose, then he nodded. "I guess that did seem suspicious, when you put it that way. I can't talk about my cases for privacy reasons, but I think I can make an exception this time. The lady was my richest client, one of Ottawa's elite citizens. She's suspected her husband of cheating for a while now, but my guys haven't been able to dig up anything, not even the tiniest piece of lint on this guy. He was leaving town unexpectedly and she specifically wanted me on the case since no one else had been able to catch him as of yet and since I'm the top gun." He shrugged modestly.

"He was already packed and in the shower when she called, so I didn't have any time to waste as he was soon leaving, going by car. I didn't even have time to go home for clothes! I ended up tailing him down to Myrtle Beach in South Carolina, a good sixteen hours away. He checked into a hotel as soon as he got there but came right back out even though we'd driven straight through the night, and off we went again to some realtor's office. This one has a happy ending though. It seems the guy was buying a house by the ocean for his wife's upcoming birthday and there had been a glitch with the paperwork, so he drove down to take care of it since her birthday is in a few days. He's been going down there, looking at properties, trying to find her the perfect place. Just to be sure though, I tailed him some more, but all he was doing was buying furniture for the house. I couldn't call or text because I hadn't been able to get my charger and my phone died. I could have gone to buy one but I had to keep an eye on the guy, so I didn't get a chance to slip away. In retrospect, though, I really should have taken half an hour to do that."

"Wow, that's actually really romantic! What a damper

the suspicion must have put on everything though. What did you tell her, so as not to ruin the surprise?"

"I told her that I could guarantee that he was not cheating on her and that the mystery would be solved in just a few days and that I staked my business on it. She seemed happy with that...she already owns a few businesses so the thought of one more brightened her up since she still didn't believe me!"

"Okay, one more thing. How did you end up being there to get me out of the trunk?"

"That, my beautiful, is a much longer story. For now, let's just say that I got back in time to help you close up the bistro, but you were missing. Your ex was there for some strange reason and was frantic about it. He claimed that he thought he heard you screaming, said he'd know that sound anywhere since you screamed at him a lot. We got the cops, and got a tip, and we went chasing after you. The rest of the story you'll get tomorrow after you get more sleep. And that's an order!" He leaned forward and kissed me to stop my protests.

My eyes flew open. "What about my parents? Why are they here?" I demanded in a panic.

"Well, I haven't been able to reach Nicole, but I did get Chloé. She called your folks when you went missing because she didn't know what else to do. They were here three hours later. Your dad even called the real estate agent this morning to see if there's any way to speed up the move since the house is empty. They convinced your brother to move into their old house so there's really nothing holding them back. I'm sorry," he looked at me sadly, knowing I wouldn't be happy with this news.

I groaned. "Hey, I thought you weren't supposed to get me agitated!"

"Agitated because your parents are moving here? Why's that such a bad thing, anyway? You never did tell me."

"Now that is a really long story," I retorted, "and you'll have to stick around a lot longer before I give you all the gory details!"

He laughed. "Why? Aren't you comfortable confiding in me?"

"No, because it will take that long to tell you all the horrors of my childhood...and I don't want to scare you away just yet!"

He gave me another soft kiss, promising to return the next day when I would likely be released. Just before leaving, he turned around and said softly, "Sorry I wasn't here for you," before slipping out the door.

My tummy did a little Zumba before I closed my eyes and took another twelve-hour nap.

CHAPTER TWENTY-FIVE

Matt was back at ten a.m. the next morning with a couple
of bags in tow. The first he laid out on the little eating tray
next to my bed. Yum! Cheese, salamis and fresh bread!
That perked me right up and we shared the meal, happily
munching in comfortable silence.

When we were done, he laid the other bag on the bed
next to me, coloring slightly and stammering, "I packed
you a bag of fresh clothes. Chloé told me where you keep
the spare keys to get up to your place since she couldn't
get the time off from her day job and she's been running
the bistro at night since we still haven't heard from
Nicole." Alarm for my missing Nicole grew.

"Oh, okay, thanks!" I said and grabbed the bag while
slowly getting out of bed to change in the small bathroom.
Once there, I understood the blush and wished the ground
would swallow me whole.

My newly purchased underwear and bras had been on
top of my older ones in my drawer, so he obviously had
just reached in and grabbed the first thing that was there:
my hot pink thong and matching silky push-up bra. I
dressed quickly then went back into the room, my own

skin blazing so hot that I thought the tips of my ears would combust. Needless to say, we avoided eye contact. Although I did eventually sneak a little peak and caught him sneaking a little peak at my bust.

Matt warned me that my parents were back at my house waiting for me and assured me that he'd fill in any remaining details back at the house.

We took a quick detour past Nicole's place. I couldn't shake the feeling that something was wrong, and when I'd called her work number, they told me she hadn't been there for a couple of days. After a few minutes of banging on the door, she finally answered, her eyes swollen and red. For the first time since I'd known her, she looked like hell.

Sniffling, she let me inside and motioned to the couch that was surrounded by a sea of wadded-up tissues. I took a spot in the least contaminated area.

Wasting no time, she dove right in: "Remember the creepy guy that I thought was following me just recently?" I nodded. "Well, he's been on the news. A lot. It seems he was involved in some type of child snatching a while back outside Toronto. He and a female accomplice were just arrested for the murder of a little blonde girl." Her voice broke and I could understand her horror. She had met the man accused of these terrible crimes and was probably lucky to still be alive. Not to mention that she had dined with the monster! "I'm so done with online dating," she mumbled.

"I'm sorry I didn't visit you in the hospital. I knew you were in good hands with Matt there and that you'd needed your rest and I really didn't want to go out looking like this! I would only have worried you and then you wouldn't have taken the time to heal," she apologized, giving me a big hug.

We talked for a few more minutes and then she ordered me to go home and rest. She'd wallow in misery for another couple of hours but promised she'd be at the bistro that night. I gave her a fierce hug and then trudged back to the car where Matt had been waiting patiently to give us some privacy.

I didn't quite know what to expect back home, but The Aliens were strangely subdued. They even attempted to speak English, which was just weird and always made me uncomfortable and I would still always answer in Hungarian.

We settled in the living room with a fresh pot of caramel coffee—a special treat from my parents—and Matt began from the beginning. Always a good idea, I suppose, since so far I'd gotten the story starting from the end.

"So, my friend Joey, the man who was killed," he elaborated for my parent's sake, "had some personal issues that had grown over the years. He was getting psychological help and had recently fallen in love for the first time ever, with Eunice. She kept trying to talk him into selling the land and from what we gather, he eventually grew suspicious and started poking around. He had a hard time believing that someone truly loved him and was convinced that she must have an ulterior motive. He was right, of course. Her partner, who was actually her real lover, killed Joey right about the time they found out you bought the bistro. They figured if they stashed Joey there, you'd be scared off and then they could buy your land too, which was part of the original plan, except their financing fell through." He paused for a few moments, overwhelmed with sadness for his late, troubled friend.

"Two of the guys who followed you were businessmen. The third guy, Jimmy, who was Eunice's cousin, ended up in your stairwell. He was responsible for all the local burglaries. Whatever he stole, he sold, and the money was supposed to go into buying the land around the trails, which was Joey's land, and yours...

"Robbing you was a bonus, since they wanted the cash and also wanted to scare you away. He started getting sloppy though, and it seems that he had developed a cocaine habit. The jumpier he became, the more nervous the other two guys and Eunice were, so they killed him during the burglary on New Years' Eve, again figuring it might convince you to put the place up for sale." He paused to make sure my parents were following. He had been speaking slowly so that they could understand, and I could tell by their expressions that they seemed to be getting the gist of it.

"But why did they start following me? Was it just to scare me?" I interrupted.

"Jimmy was supposed to get into your place and trash things up but he was high and had his own ideas and thought a short cut would work. He threw the rock through your window figuring it might be enough to scare you. It would seem that nothing scared you off though." He beamed at me with pride for a moment. "Then, after he was killed, the other two guys thought they might have lost a lighter in here and were afraid one of their prints might be on it, plus it was engraved with Fred's initials. He was Eunice's real boyfriend. Already though, when you paid the surprise visit to Joey's house the first time, Eunice was freaked out, so they were sure you were on to them."

"I should have figured it out," I admitted. "She'd been packing boxes, saying she was helping Joey get rid of stuff. A true hoarder, though, wouldn't be comfortable with someone else getting rid of his stuff without being able to supervise it and have a say about each and every item going into a box or into the trash. I missed that clue. So why did bozo and bozo come here with beards the other night?"

"They were listening and watching, seeing if they could hear any tidbits of information and also with the lights and candles on, they figured maybe they'd spot the lighter. I'm guessing that maybe they saw it because they broke in and got it, right?"

"That's right...but I may have played a hand in that," I

replied sheepishly. "I had placed some calls to people who'd been here on New Years' Eve and had gotten into a conversation about a missing lighter. I told the person I had found it, sensing that there was more to the story, so then I went out and bought one. When they broke in though, they found the real one that I hadn't actually known about. But why did that guy patch up my broken window?"

Matt shook his head in disbelief at my admission of playing detective. "Well, he was kind of embarrassed by that. Seems that Buddy—and that's actually his name—has been going along with everything and he felt bad about everything. He really used to be a respectable businessman, and nothing rough was supposed to happen."

I snorted in disgust. "Okay, so then why come here the night of the murder mystery dinner?"

"Simple. Greedy for one, and now that Fred had his lighter back, he was going to silence you, since he and Eunice were convinced you knew about them. Only Buddy didn't know about that part of the plan. They figured they were safe and thought they were clever with the beards on. The guy that was left behind, Buddy, thought it was only going to be another robbery, and figured that you'd make a ton of cash that night and they could help themselves to it, since the window on your back door was still broken. He made sure that I'd tell you that he never meant for you to get hurt in any way and didn't know that you would."

My temper flared and I made a mental note to definitely change that back door to a metal one with no window.

Matt continued: "What I can't quite figure, and neither could Buddy, is how you pieced it all together and recognized them? He said you had a funny look on your face and there was no question that you knew something, but they weren't sure what and why, and thought maybe you'd marked the bills or something and they hadn't noticed."

I smiled. My *aha* moment. "It's your fault, really. Remember when you wrote your name and number on a bill and gave it to me? That bill was stolen the first time around. The idiot used that money to pay me, so he gave me back my own money."

We shared a grin then Matt continued. "Yes, I remember. You were so beautiful that night," he murmured huskily. He glanced quickly at my parents, remembering we weren't alone in the room and cleared his throat. "Okay, makes sense. So next, they figured out that you were on to them in their disguises and Buddy insisted on leaving. Fred, the one that's been doing the killing, said he has to go to the can first. Instead, he went back to your kitchen, beat the crap out of you and stole you with the help of Eunice, who was waiting out back with the car. As a parting gift to himself, he snagged your cash bag, which was right on the counter.

"They left poor Buddy back there in the restaurant waiting since they'd all come in one car. Everyone had cleared out and he was out front, still waiting, when the cops showed up. He was like a deer caught in headlights, and of course Nicole remembered you talking about the guys with the beards, so she got the cops on him. He was so pissed at Fred and Eunice for taking off on him and leaving him in the spotlight that he told everything he knew. He told us where Fred lived and about a cabin the guy had, so some cops headed out to the house and the rest of us headed for the cabin, figuring that would be his destination."

"And is that where he'd stopped when the Behemoth was trying to get me out of the trunk?" I asked. Matt laughed at my pet name for the girl.

"No, he pulled over at an old car repair shop on a side road that was closed at that time of night. They just wanted to bash your head in a few more times for fun and leave you there to die. They knew their luck had run out, so they were leaving town.

"So, dat bastarrrd is going to jail?" my dad asked, speaking for the first time.

"Oh yes, no doubt about that. There is definitely nothing to worry about anymore. He's going to jail, and Eunice died instantly in the crash." With that, he took my hand and began doing those crazy little thumb rubs that make me feel all squishy.

"So I guess Leonardo or Janet didn't have anything to do with this?" I was still puzzled by those two.

"Janet?" my father asked. "Vy you thinking Janet?"

"Well, she had access to the house and seemed nervous by it all and then she disappeared for a while, and it seems she was interested in the property, too. Are we sure she's not part of it?"

"Definitely not. The cops had checked her out. She was gone on vacation recently and when she came back and spoke with you, she got more nervous. She went to the police after your last talk and told them about how the two properties were connected by trails and that she'd heard some potential clients talk about future investments, bulldozing Joey's place and this one, and putting a Bed and Breakfast place at both ends, that type of thing. They didn't know she'd heard and she wanted to stay out of it since she's got a young kid at home and didn't want to be involved, but in the end she knew she had to step forward. She couldn't remember which client it was, since it had been a while ago, so the cops were going through the list of people who'd visited the house."

"And Leonardo?"

"Ah, good old Mr. Leonardo: he just hates you. There's nothing more to it than that."

"That's comforting," I sighed. "And what about the former owners?"

"Same thing, just bitter that they had to go out of business and that you seem to be doing well. Mind you, they were friends with Leonardo until he opened the pizza joint. And I suspect the lady may have had an affair with him, but I'm still not too clear about that. That was just some gossip going around town that I'd picked up."

I shuddered at the mental image and remembered her story about Leonardo walking in on her when she was bathing. Likely there was more to that story than she let on, especially since I'd seen them together in the restaurant downtown.

Finally, "My ex? What's his story? Why does he keep showing up here?" My parents gasped at the mention of Hans.

"The last time that I saw him in your lot I told him to take a hike or we'd get a restraining order against him. I figured he was just jealous that you finally opened your own place and he figured you'd be rolling in money and that you'd eventually pay him off to leave you alone. But then he was here the night you got kidnapped and he seemed pretty frantic to me. I'm thinking he's not quite over you yet and just has a funny way of showing it." Matts' grip on my hand tightened a little.

I grimaced at the thought of Hans still in love with me and then stewed awhile, but then I was distracted by the thumb moving round and round on my hand. I took a deep breath.

"Okay, Mom and Dad, stop worrying about me. I love you and I'm really happy to see you both and I really appreciate you coming to take care of me. Since we'll practically be neighbors, I guess we'll be spending lots more time together so we may as well get a few things settled right now. I'm a grown-up, I'm thirty years old, I have a life now and sometimes, I might even have sex." Matt and my parents gasped and I quickly continued before I lost my nerve. "Not right this minute, of course, but eventually. Definitely eventually. So, if you see a car here at night sometimes, and I didn't invite you over, then don't come over. Am I clear?"

I looked around the room and no one spoke for a minute. Finally my mother broke the ice as she stood and walked over to Matt and said, "I give Matt pussy." To this day I still recall the horrified look on his face and I practically pee myself from laughing when I think of it.

She stood in front of him smiling. My dad and I were laughing so hard I could barely spit out the words. "Pussy in Hungarian is a kiss, Matt. It's spelled different but that's how it's pronounced."

Relieved, he grinned and stood up, allowing my mother to kiss his cheek and to thank him for protecting me. Next, it was my turn.

I took him by the hand and told my parents we'd be downstairs in the bistro for a while. We managed to find a quiet corner for two as another couple had just left. Nicole and Chloé waved from across the room and Nicole gave me the 'just a minute' finger. In turn, I gave her the 'shoo fly' hand—no thanks, we're good.

Turning to face Matt, I leaned forward for a long kiss. When we came up for air, he angled his head to speak into my ear. "You've got a whole drawer full of thongs, and I want to see each and every one of them."

My cheeks blazed at the reminder but having boldly informed my parents that I intended to have sex, I couldn't back down now. With a Mona Lisa smile, I whispered a suggestion.

EPILOGUE

I stood, admiring the new heavy duty metal door that had just been installed at the back of my bistro. Ha, I chortled to myself, no one's going to break in now. It was hard to believe that the events that had led to this new door started only a short month and a half ago.

Just then, it burst open and a scraggly guy scowled at me. I only had time to note that he was wearing a ball cap; nothing unusual around these parts.

"Gimme all your cash," he demanded, his hands balled into fists.

I snorted, "I haven't been open in days, I have no money." We glared at each other. "Here; have a sandwich," I said, shoving a plate his way.

With another glare, he snatched the food and ran. Huh, I sighed. I should probably keep the door locked.

MEXICAN ROLL UPS

Just as easy as the ham pitas.

    1 cup plain cream cheese
    3/4 cup salsa (whatever kind you like)
    1 cup shredded cheese (whatever kind you like)
    1 finely chopped green onions including the green
    bits (I'm told these are called scallions in some places)
    Dash of dill- optional. I use it in everything

Mix. Spread on your tortillas of choice. Roll up, wrap in
plastic wrap. Freeze if you're not using it right away.
When ready to serve, take out of freezer. Should be ready
to cut into 1 inch pieces within 30 minutes. It is best
served just slightly frozen.

Do you want More "Whine and Cheese?" *Ice-wine and Irish Cheddar* is the second cozy mystery in the series and will be published in October 2016 by Open Books.

THANK YOU

*Th*ank you to everyone who has purchased my book. If it doesn't lighten your mood and make you chuckle, I have not accomplished my goal.

Four personal thank you's are also in order;

Cassandra Ritchie, for being my guinea pig and editing the very first draft of my book, raising questions for loose ends and politely pointing out errors. I am indebted to you.

My son Kyle Farrell, for his support and helping me out around the house when there just weren't enough hours in a day to get everything done. And best of all, when he told me he was proud of me.

Paul Dehnert, the anchoring rock in my life, for his gentle encouragement to contact more publishers and reminders that I should be writing, as well as his constant enthusiasm, pride, support and strength.

Last but not least, my parents, for raising me Hungarian and giving me a great foundation for the book. Side note, like Amalia in the book, I never did go into accounting.

Cheers, my friends.